Praise for *Two*

"..."Two Times Removed" is a book woman in your life. It's cerebral, unadulterated, and reads like a love offering. Each featured author brings a unique Indo Caribbean flavour to the pages of "Two Times Removed," every word worth your attention. The book is proof enough of why it rests on us to document the narratives of our people."
—*Brown Girl Magazine*

"The writers traverse their worlds as they delve into their identities, family, trauma, relationships and more as children raised in the Indo-Caribbean diaspora. Tiara Jade Chutkhan is of Guyanese and Trinidadian roots. She is the editor-in-chief of Brown Girl Diary, which focuses on the representation of Indo-Caribbean women... Her writing offers a voice and empowerment to those who haven't felt, seen or are confident enough to express their culture."
—*The Caribbean Camera*

"As someone with an Indo-Caribbean background, it's so refreshing to read stories that I relate to. Growing up, it was rare to come across literature or any media that depicted the culture that I was raised in. This book allowed me to feel seen in a way that I never imagined. It goes above and beyond in representing our culture, history, and resilience as a group of people."
—*Denisha Nandkumar, Amazon Reviewer*

"It was such a pleasure sitting down and indulging in fiction written by authors of my own heritage. Being a part of West Indian literature is such an honour, even if it's just as a reader. Every story in this anthology had a sense of reality, passion, and a deep-rooted and explored love for our people, our culture, and our history... Overall, excellent work on these stories. Thank you to all the authors for being brave and transparent with their stories. Even in fiction, there is truth."
—*Nievana Judisthir*

TWO TIMES REMOVED

TWO TIMES REMOVED

An Anthology of Contemporary Indo-Caribbean Stories

VOLUME II

Edited and Curated by

Tiara Jade Chutkhan

Bookworm
PUBLISHING

Two Times Removed

Volume II

Copyright © 2022 Tiara Jade Chutkhan

First paperback edition June 2022

Book design by Chelsi Bhagan
Stories contributed by Saira Batasar, Anna Maria Chowthi, Tiara Jade Chutkhan, Chelsea
DeBarros, Michelle DeFreitas, Amanda Dejesus, Aaron Ishmael, Joshua Timothy Jaipaul, Jamie
Langford, Nalini Mahadeo, Jaimini Mangrue, Alyssa Mongroo, Alisha Persaud, Nadia Persaud,
Savita Prasad, Anjali Seegobin, Samantha Raghunandan and Angelica Razack-Francis

ISBN: 978-1-7777274-3-7 (paperback)
ISBN: 978-1-7777274-4-4 (eBook)
ISBN: 978-1-7777274-5-1 (hardcover)

www.tiarajade.com

For the Indo-Caribbean storytellers of the past, present and future. Your words are more valuable than you'll ever know.

For the Indo-Caribbean community, which has continued to support and uplift this project. Words will never be enough to explain how grateful I am.

For the ancestors, we know and don't know. Your sacrifices will never go unnoticed; we carry you with us and will continue to make you proud.

For the Indo-Caribbean men and women who strive to create representation and resources for our community. You are changing history each day.

For each of the talented contributors of this book, and the last. These works could never have come to life without you. Thank you for sharing your stories with me. It has been an honour and privilege.

Contents

"You take a capsule from India, leave it here for a hundred years, and this is what you get."—**Mungal Patasar**

"If you look deeply into the palm of your hand, you will see your parents and all the generations of your ancestors. All of them are alive in this moment. Each is present in your body. You are the continuation of each of these people."— **Thich Nhat Hanh**

Introduction

Two times removed. We are two times removed. It has been almost 200 years since people of East Indian descent first set foot on Caribbean soil to work the sugar plantations. The first ships carrying *indentured labourers*, the Whitby and Hesperus, left the ports of Calcutta in 1838, just four years after the abolition of slavery. These ships were bound for British Guiana, what we know today as Guyana. It carried 396 passengers, of which 22 were women. Most of the people immigrating would have come from the regions of Uttar Pradesh and western Bihar, but small numbers from Punjab and Bangladesh were aboard as well. In the years that followed, East Indians were brought to work on five and 10 year contracts in Trinidad & Tobago, Jamaica, Grenada, Guyana, St. Lucia and Martinique to name a few. The system of indenture lasted almost 80 years, during which 500,000 East Indians came to the Caribbean. It was abolished in 1917.

Upon their arrival, indentured workers were given one set of clothes, cooking supplies, and rations of food. They were then transported to their assigned plantations, beginning work immediately. The work day began at sunrise and ended at sunset. These men and women did their best to settle into their new lives despite harsh conditions and the realization that they would be living a life far different than the dream they were sold. Resilient as ever, they pushed on, laying the necessary bricks for the future of their families. Small numbers returned to India at the end of their terms, but were often outcasted by the communities they left. Some then returned back to the Caribbean and settled in the islands with larger Indian communities. It was in this new space the men and women of indenture, our foremothers and forefathers, created a new identity. Today we call ourselves Indo-Caribbeans.

Storytelling has always been an integral part of Indo-Caribbean culture. Onboard indenture ships, amongst their *jahaji,* Indian men and women sang songs and shared stories from home to pass time during the long voyages. In the Caribbean, sitting around makeshift kitchens, sharing simple meals after a long day under the hot sun, they shared news and folktales. Historically, the average person did not know how to read or write. The ancient practice of oral storytelling was not only part of our ancestors' traditions, but the way they shared information and passed down folktales, myths, epic fantasies, and of course, history. For centuries it was the primary vessel in exchanging these stories from generation to generation, ensuring their survival. The storytellers were highly respected and valued in villages. Through voice and body language, they would animate the tales for their audience, bringing them to life in any space at any time of day.

There are pieces of our history, due to colonialism and lack of resources, that haven't survived the test of time. While there is plenty of information documented and available to us, as well as many researchers, archivists and historians who have dedicated their lives to preservation, there are gaps in existing archives. Many documents and records have begun to disintegrate due to lack of proper care. What has been particularly important to the survival of our ancestors' stories as well as documenting those of recent generations are books.

In the 20th century, an influx of Indo-Caribbean literature was published, with names like V.S. Naipaul, Harold Sonny Ladoo, Cyril Dabydeen, Shani Mootoo, Mahadai Das, Ramabai Espinet, Ron Ramdin and countless others creating a literary legacy that defined our identity and experiences. These works told stories of Indo-Caribbean people post-indenture, exploring family dynamics and gender roles, the political climate in the islands, immigration, and traumas. I will never forget the period in my life when I discovered how many Indo-Caribbean books were actually out there. I had stumbled across a list on the Indo-Caribbean Alliance website and to this day I will always liken that moment to striking gold. For me, and I believe many others, my introduction to Indo-Caribbean literature started with *Coolie Woman* by Gaiutra Bahadur. Soon after, I got my hands on titles like *Secrets We Kept, Trauma, Jahaji, Miguel Street, The Swinging Bridge* and *He Drown She in the Sea*. The people and characters in these books reflected my family and I whether it was through the way they spoke, how they looked, the struggles they faced, or sacrifices they made. Since then my collection has continued to grow, and one section of my bookshelf is now proudly dedicated to my Indo-Caribbean books.

It was the feeling that first set of books gave me that inspired the first *Two Times Removed* book. Having read and understood the stories of our past, I felt that there was a place where our history trailed off. We understood the system of indenture, and experiences of our ancestors; we explored life in the Caribbean in the decades after abolition and the challenges our people faced. We knew the stories of our parents, many of whom had immigrated abroad. Now there is a generation of Indo-Caribbeans who were born and raised in North America—first-generation Canadians and Americans. We are the first Indo-Caribbeans who have grown up exclusively in this North American society, raised by parents who grew up in the islands and did their best to preserve the feeling of "home" while trying to fit into this new world. We are the generation that sought out a deeper connection to the lands we didn't know; we yearned for a deeper connection to our culture and history. We are the generation that is Two Times Removed.

When *Two Times Removed* was first released in May 2021, I couldn't have imagined the reaction it would gather. In the past few years I have watched our community grow; our voices have become louder and we are taking up space in a positive way. There are multiple platforms doing amazing work for our community whether it's sharing history and informative content, hosting workshops and events, or providing resources. Many of us are working to heal generational traumas and unlearn the mentalities that no longer serve us. We are working to give future generations the tools and support we didn't have until recent times.

As someone who didn't grow up with many Indo-Caribbean people outside of my family, I truly love seeing this. I love that regardless of where we are in the world, Indo-Caribbean people can connect and support one another. *Two Times Removed* has been a perfect example of this. Working on these projects has allowed me the privilege of connecting with Indo-Caribbean writers across North America, but also readers from all across the world. I am both humbled and grateful to have received feedback from readers who felt seen and represented through *Two Times Removed*, but also found it healing and therapeutic to read.

I am always very transparent about the time in my life when this series first came to mind; I wasn't in school, I had been let go from my seasonal retail job, and had just gotten involved with Brown Gyal Diary. I wasn't sure what career I wanted to pursue, and I'd just begun my own personal journey of exploring my Indo-Caribbean identity. As I think many young people can relate, we go through times where, to put it plainly, nothing makes sense. We question our life purpose, wonder if we're doing the right thing, and for children of immigrants, we bear the weight of wanting to make our families proud. We carry this weight on our shoulders and push on, knowing that we mustn't let their struggles and sacrifices be in vain.

In reading and editing the stories in the first volume, I learned that others struggled with the same things that I had throughout my life; identity, family relationships, connecting to my roots, mental health. *Two Times Removed* made me feel seen and represented in a way that had yet to be done. It inspired me to seek answers to questions that had loomed in my head for years. As you will later see, my piece is about finding my paternal grandfather, a man I had never known nor even seen a photo of all my life. In the past year I connected with several people including my grandfather's ex-wife and his sisters, met new family members, and discovered pieces of the past that I never would've known about if not for taking the chance and asking those difficult questions.

The work in this anthology is deeply personal to each of the contributors, as they have opened up about vulnerable parts of their lives or written stories with characters that are in vulnerable places. In this volume we are speaking up on issues such as anti-Blackness in the Indo-Caribbean community in Savita Prasad's *Shades of Caramel* and gender based violence in the Caribbean in Alyssa Mongroo's *Life Goes On*. We are shedding light on taboo topics such as infertility in Saira Batasar Johnie's *Being Indo-Caribbean and the Realities of Infertility in Canadian Context* and seeking help when struggling with mental health in Anjali Seegobin's *Mad*. It is for these reasons I believe this volume in particular carries so much value.

It is my sincerest wish that every reader will see themselves, their family, their friends and community represented as they read the stories in this book; that they will find comfort in the people and characters, and perhaps, healing. I hope this book can be shared with loved ones and the stories within can help to spark conversations on the topics they explore.

I often get messages from people who are contemplating sharing their stories, and if you are currently in this position, I hope this book will inspire you to take a chance on yourself and write the story you feel compelled to tell. Our words are powerful, and hold more value than we often know. We have the ability to create timeless work and continue the legacies that first began decades ago.

As editor of this volume, it is my honour to present readers this newest volume in the *Two Times Removed* series.

Being Indo-Caribbean and the Realities of Infertility in the Canadian Context

Saira Batasar-Johnie

Trigger warning mentions miscarriage, loss, pregnancy

When you get married or make the decision to spend the rest of your life with someone, you begin to dream about your future together. Your growth in your respective careers, seeing the world together, the couch potato moments you'll experience, becoming parents together (should you choose to have children), evolving and growing together. I know this is what I did when I knew my partner was the one for me.

Growing up, I was always one to love children. I was that older cousin who enjoyed playing with all my younger cousins, who was drawn to the new babies and just wanted to hold them. I was the aunty who would plan birthday parties and games. I also loved talking to pregnant bellies; I found them so fascinating and thought the women who were carrying them seemed superhuman. Children have so much light within them; this is likely why I chose to work with children and youth as my career. Little did I know that I would experience my own struggle and trauma in trying to create these small humans that I loved so much.

Growing up in an Indo-Caribbean home, the body was not spoken about. I remember having a heavy period for the first time with excessive cramps. My mom gave me a pad and told me it wasn't really my period and said they would teach me about this in school. The pain continued in my cycles, and I was eventually diagnosed with a hormonal imbalance and given birth control to solve it; this was not an option. Instead, my mother's response was, "She can take Tylenol." That was the end of the conversation regarding my reproductive health. This was also just the beginning of a journey I knew nothing about until adulthood.

***

When I met my partner, I knew I wanted to marry him, create a life with him, have children, raise a little family, and grow old together. We talked in the early days about how many kids we each wanted. I wanted four; he wanted two. I've always loved the idea of having a big family and big family dinners because, despite being from a big family and having five siblings myself, we never had those memorable moments due to family differences. My partner and I had a conversation before we got married: he asked if we could start having children right away, given that he has Crohn's disease and we didn't know how long it would take us to conceive. Initially, I had wanted to wait a couple of years to enjoy married life, but I was open to the idea. We got married and signed our names on the dotted line. He was mine.

We were able to get pregnant right away, *pregnancy number one*, but that happiness was quickly taken away when we experienced our first loss on Thanksgiving long weekend. I had a gut feeling something else was wrong; we were timing my ovulation, doing what google said to do when Trying to Conceive (TTC), and still nothing. I booked an appointment with my family doctor and let him know about my concerns. I may have fibbed a bit to be able to be referred to a fertility clinic because I did not want to wait (typically, you must be TTC for a year before being referred to a fertility clinic).

While waiting for the phone call to begin the process, we were both going through a lot of emotions; moving in together for the first time and getting to know one another. Our routines made it exciting and stressful as we seemed to argue about everything. This began our journey of therapy and thank goodness we did it because we came from such different families and upbringings. Learning each other's communication styles and love language was our biggest task to understand. We've been together now for 12 years, and we are stronger than ever, thanks to the therapists we have experienced.

The call eventually came for our consultation appointment, marking the beginning of the long journey ahead of us. We attended the appointment to book more appointments, semen analysis, sonogram, blood work for both of us, AMH blood work, and cycle tracks. I remember thinking, *what does this all mean?* There was so much information all at once. I felt overwhelmed, but hopeful, and so was he.

We completed all the bloodwork and tests, resulting in me being diagnosed with PolyCystic Ovarian Syndrome and Thyroid issues. My partner has a lower sperm count than the average male. What was next? We decided to do cycle monitoring, but each month turned out to be a disappointment. I did not understand why my body wouldn't do the one thing I wanted it to.

Not knowing many people who have gone through the fertility process made it quite lonely. Watching my friends, family and coworkers get pregnant, attending their baby showers and putting on that happy face for two hours, but crying in my car after the fact, asking why not me? Being Indo-Caribbean and struggling with infertility is yet another topic you just don't discuss or ask questions about. Instagram was not as popular, and Google wasn't always helpful. I had a couple of coworkers going through a similar process, so I looked to them for guidance and support while attending my appointments and hearing results that I didn't understand. I remember sitting at the dinner table with my mom and sister and telling them what we were going through. My sister had then shared that she had experienced a loss before she had my niece. My mom shared that I was a fertility clinic baby and in the 1990s, the process was very different. She referred to my father's sperm as soldiers; apparently, he had many they just did not swim. Hearing their experiences was comforting. I felt a sense of hope, but this was our only conversation about what I was going through.

Our fertility clinic doctor put my partner on vitamins to increase his sperm count and I was put on Clomid, a drug that helps you to ovulate more than one egg a cycle to increase your chances of hopefully implanting one of them. I attended monthly transvaginal ultrasound appointments and got blood work drawn between 6- 7 a.m. before heading to work with a smile on my face.

After trying naturally with cycle monitoring, we decided to try Intrauterine Insemination (IUI) a step before IVF. I had two follicles (which release eggs) growing on my right ovary. We were able to conceive our son through this process. Many people have asked me what IUI is: it is essentially the clinic washing your partner's sperm and putting it into a syringe. The syringe has a thin tube attached to it, so it can be inserted into your cervix. Then the next step is as if you are having a pap test done with a little clamp.

You then lay there for 15-20 minutes. I did this process twice back-to-back, and we were able to get a healthy egg and healthy sperm.

Pregnancy number two. Conceiving our first rainbow baby, our son, was a journey, but we weren't aware of the next journey we had ahead of us. We were grateful, thankful and so appreciative of him. We knew we wanted to continue to have kids, just not right after having him. Despite just giving birth, the questions and comments of "When you go have a next one?" and "Don't wait too long" started. I didn't realize how much they impacted me until we were ready to begin the process of trying again.

Once we were ready to begin exploring the idea of having another baby, we were able to get pregnant, but then we lost *miscarriage number two.* Six weeks later, *pregnancy number three.* This was devastating, but to be expected. Given what we knew based on our history, we decided to go back to our previous fertility clinic. The doctor ran additional blood work on us, one being a Karyotype test. We received the news we weren't expecting and I was diagnosed with a Pericentric Inversion on Chromosome 16. This meant my chromosome 16 in my eggs was flipped, and once inseminated by my partner's sperm, it would most likely miscarry if it were not a "Healthy Egg," and my body would reject it. On top of everything else my body was dealing with when it came to fertility, I was now diagnosed with this. I went home and held my son a little longer. What were our options? The doctor said we could continue to try naturally and continue to miscarry until we got a healthy egg, which was emotionally taxing. We also had the option of IUI, but there was no way of knowing if I would ovulate a healthy egg. We could spend $25,000 to $30,00,0, most likely more, to complete In-vitro Fertilization (IVF). We would have to test each egg to see if it was a healthy egg. For example, they could take out 10 eggs from my ovaries, and if from those 10, five eggs qualify as good for insemination, it will cost around $2500 per egg to test. We are making a gamble from those five– all of them could have the pericentric inversion and we wouldn't know until it is inseminated. That is just one cycle of IVF.

After digesting all this information, we were referred to a genetic clinic to discuss my inversion more in-depth. Not long after, we found out we were pregnant again, *pregnancy number four.* We tried to be optimistic about this pregnancy. We saw a strong heartbeat and curry became my enemy again, but my symptoms started to disappear and we lost this baby at 10 weeks. I was told by the ultrasound tech, "You are so young. You still have time." Little did she know what I was diagnosed with or how badly I wanted this small human.

I had lost this baby around the first anniversary of my father's passing. I was a hot mess. I felt like I was being punished. I would go to work and cry in my office. I felt alone. My inversion was uncommon, and finding a support system of people to understand what I was going through was difficult. When I tried to confide in those close to me, they would either share their losses or tell me to be grateful I have a child. "You should just be one and done" (please don't say this to someone who has dreams of wanting more children). We were grateful to have had our son, but I wasn't ready to come to terms with the idea of not being able to have more children. I hit my breaking point, and so I went back to therapy for myself because I had no idea how to cope.

My husband and I attended a meeting with a genetic counsellor to explain my inversion further. It could have been passed on, or I could be DiNovo, meaning in the utero, it just created itself. We left with more information to process. I picked up medication from my fertility clinic; this time, I was given Misoprostol, a drug that helps/forces a woman's body to expel the contents in her uterus. Usually, I would just start bleeding, but not with this one. I felt my cervix opening and this small grape leaving me. It was an extremely emotional period in my life, so I decided to take a break and re-evaluate everything in my life; the people I surrounded myself with, the goals I had for myself, work on my marriage and work on being present as a mom. I took the time to myself that I needed after loss after loss. It's a lot of trauma on one's body.

While making this decision, we decided that we would try a different fertility clinic because our final meeting with our doctor had been a negative experience. We had attended a meeting with the doctor, and a different patient's name called me; I read the wrong file and he just overall looked tired. I understood that people get burned out, but we were coming to doctors for support and should've been treated with dignity and respect, just as everyone else attending these clinics should be.

***

The Covid-19 pandemic stopped the world and started our discussion to try again. The pandemic was a blessing for us, as we needed to slow down and appreciate what we had. Our little family thrived together. *Pregnancy number five* came as fast as it left. My cousin had told me about a holistic fertility clinic doctor that believed in working with naturopaths and vitamins to support egg health and sperm health, so we journeyed to our third fertility clinic. We were waitlisted for three months and decided to continue with TTC. I got a call for an appointment the same week I found out I was pregnant again, *pregnancy number six*. At this point, I became numb to feeling any sort of excitement or happiness when I would see those two lines. We went forward with the appointment, had my dating ultrasound, and saw a heartbeat. July 15th, 2021, was the predicted due date. It's crazy to think that in 2021 I had three different due dates due to three different pregnancies.

I met with the fertility clinic doctor alone. Because of COVID-19, partners weren't allowed to be present anymore. I was put on vitamins. I noticed my symptoms starting to fade during week 10. I went to the hospital, had no heartbeat, and started bleeding. My body had started the process of expelling the fetus on its own. I felt like I was in mini labour, feeling my cervix open, the cramping, the constant running to the washroom to push. 24 hours of that and it was over. Again, my little grape had left my body a week before Christmas. I felt empty again.

I must praise my partner throughout this process. He has been my rock, person, everything, and more. He's supported me, let me cry on him, and has just sat in silence with me when I needed it. The process of loss can be lonely, but with him by my side, I did not feel like I was going through this by myself. This is something we wanted together; therefore, we went through every step together.

During my loss, I was connected to an amazing human whom I call today a blessing. Dr. Jessica Dupont is a naturopath specializing in women's health and specifically helps women get pregnant, stay pregnant, and carry to term. I signed up for her fertility cleanse, determined to learn about my body and what I needed to do to help me be the best version of myself to carry a baby again and ovulate a healthy egg. While doing this, I started taking vitamins, changed the way I ate, and my fertility clinic wanted to have me try a drug that would increase my ovulation. The needles began, along with the bruises on my tummy and tons and tons of expenses. Insurance companies are not the greatest in understanding fertility drugs and having to advocate and educate them was draining. Had I not advocated for us as a couple, we would have been paying over $3000 out of pocket for the needles I was required to take. No one will understand what it is like going to a fertility clinic unless they have lived it. Going through the intrusiveness of having a vaginal ultrasound in deafening silence, not being told what's happening to you or your body, laying there exposed to a stranger, bare-legged and widespread. You stay in silence, staring at a screen displaying an empty womb, but hope that maybe there's an equipment technical error. This was the process that I had been going through for the past four years on and off.

We finally decided we wanted to try IVF. We would use our savings and try one last time, exhausting all of our options before we stopped. Our doctor convinced us to try IUI first to again monitor the drugs and the dosage she needed to give me to get the best results. I worked with my naturopath and began acupuncture while continuing my fertility detox diet and manifesting this small human. I would talk to my uterus, do ovary and uterus massages, and get my partner involved every step of the way. I would close my eyes as he administered my needles in the morning (I am sure he closed his eyes the first time he gave me my needle with the ovulation drug). Despite the doctor having to take my blood monthly for fertility purposes, I still was not used to needles. I bruised, it sucked, but it worked. I was ovulating two follicles, meaning two eggs were growing.

We set a date for my IUI procedure. It felt lonely this time. When I did IUI to have my first son, my partner was able to be with me in the room. My naturopath recommended I play something to remind me of him, so I listened to our wedding song on repeat. IUI is yet another very intrusive procedure, as I described above. We were done five minutes after they inserted his sperm from a tube into my uterus. I lay there for 15 minutes, praying and talking out loud to empty space. *Please help his sperm meet a healthy egg. Please, just please, help us. I hope this will be our last time through this process.*

I went for my acupuncture with my naturopath and then headed home to rest and wait two weeks. In addition to waiting, my doctor had given me progesterone suppositories as additional support to help with implantation. I started peeing on sticks, but nothing. Day 10 came; I peed on a stick and saw a faint line, two lines. I did the same thing the next morning. The second line got darker. I went to my clinic, did blood work, and my Human Chorionic Gonadotropin (HCG) hormone numbers were high. *Pregnancy number seven* began. I went for my first ultrasound and saw an empty womb and a growing sac. My heart sank yet again.

"Looks like you can get pregnant, but not produce anything," said the ultrasound tech.

I always wondered why there are such insensitive humans that make hurtful comments to women. My doctor wanted to wait one more week. I agreed. My partner remained hopeful, but I struggled. A week passed, HCG still rising, I went for my ultrasound, and there we saw a little blob floating with a strong heartbeat. I was in disbelief, but I started praying. I called my partner and sent him pictures. November 13th, 2021, was our predicted due date, also my partner's birthday. I continued my acupuncture, took my vitamins, and experienced horrible morning sickness. I was so scared to get excited that I cried a lot. I didn't know how to feel. We made it past 10 weeks and past 12 weeks, and we soon made it to the second trimester. Still so much risk, but this was our first time getting to this point since our son. The entire pregnancy was terrifying, there were moments when I felt so happy and excited, but fear would overcome my body. The trauma of losing so many before this baby made me incredibly fragile emotionally. The only thing that helped me get through the pregnancy was prayer and talking to the baby. Being pregnant during a pandemic is terrifying. You do everything alone; appointments, ultrasounds, and tests. I tried to involve my partner as much as I could through the process.

We were blessed with our second son in October 2021, right before the fourth wave of the pandemic in Ontario. We faced some challenges with postpartum care, but he was beautiful and healthy. Our prayers were finally answered.

***

You can support someone going through their own infertility journey by just being present for them, letting them share with you, and genuinely listening to them. There were so many times I just wanted a friend to listen to me, but instead, they began sharing their own experience or telling me they knew a friend who went through the same thing. No experience is exactly the same. It completely took away from my experience. Here are some phrases or comments that I experienced during my journey that I would strongly recommend you don't say to someone struggling.

Things not to say to a friend or family member when struggling with infertility:

"At least you can get pregnant."

"Just stop stressing."

"I have a friend who struggled too. She and her partner got really drunk and she got pregnant."

"It will happen in time; your body is just overworked."

"Just be one and done."

"Be grateful you have one child; some people don't even have one."

"Jeez, you make this process sound so exhausting. Just have fun."

"When do you have kids?"

"When do you have more kids?"

"Don't wait too long."

"Your eggs will get old."

"Your son wants a sibling; why are you guys waiting so long?"

"You are so young; you have so much time."

"God has a plan for you."

"God wouldn't give you more than you can handle."

I know I am guilty of saying some of these comments above before I knew the struggle of going through infertility. I have experienced these comments myself, some by well-educated folks and it's completely hurtful and disheartening. It's so important to have a strong support team that can lift you up after some of those bad days.

Things you can say to support a friend or family member when they struggle with infertility:

"That sounds like a lot to go through; how can I support you through this?"

"I am here if you need someone to listen to you."

"What can I do at this moment?"

"How are you managing through all of this?"

"How is your partner doing? Do you folks need food?"

"This sounds incredibly difficult. I can't imagine what it must be like, but I am here for you."

"I care about you."

"Would you like to go for a walk, out for tea, sit on the phone in silence? Anything you need, we can do."

It is also so important that if you are close friends with someone who is struggling with loss and you get pregnant, you tell them before you make the announcement, especially if they are someone close to you. Of course, we are happy for you, but we are sad for us because we wish it could be us sharing the news as well. You must give them time to process and let them reach out to you on their own time.

***

There are unspoken feelings that I find women don't talk about. I find myself uncomfortable saying them out loud as well; maybe that's why. As soon as my son could start talking, he asked for a sibling. He watched his friends and cousins have little brothers and sisters and he wondered why not him. I still remember a moment we shared in his jujitsu changing room. There were two brothers with their mom, and my son turned to me and asked, "Why don't I have a little brother or sister? Did I do something wrong?" I remember looking down as tears filled my eyes because I had just experienced a loss and I told him we just have to pray and the universe/God will bless us one day. I told him he was perfect and that he did nothing wrong. How do you respond to that while you are grieving your losses? How do you not get angry with your body because it won't do something you've been asking it to do? How do you not feel like a failure? Feel incompetent? Feel stressed when everyone around you is asking you/telling you not to wait too long? There is so much shame, heaviness, and pressure that women deal with and emotions that are difficult to process, yet we continue to carry on.

Being Indo-Caribbean, I am so grateful to be a part of a beautiful Caribbean community. We still have a long way to go. There is still so much work we must do to learn, teach and unlearn. I hope that women continue to share their stories as infertility is still heavily stigmatized in our community and told not to discuss or share with others because of the shame and "What would people say" mindset. My journey has been long, painful, and an emotional rollercoaster, but it has come to an end because I have been blessed with two beautiful small humans. I hope sharing this journey will be helpful to others.

Remember, the loss is loss; never let anyone minimize your pain.

Gold: Indo-Caribbean Resilience and Healing

Anna Maria Chowthi

Chapter 1: Nahi
Leaving by choice or not

Heavy the basin upon her head
Corns on her feet, pasted on like glue

Panee trips off her body,
Enough for the thirsty village children
Begging for more.

You! Come! Gold!
Nahi! Nahi! Nahi!
Yes, you! Come! Gold!
Nahi! Nahi! Nahi!

Chapter 2: Jahaji
Crossing the dark ocean

Ek. Do. Teen. Char. Punch.
One hour, two days, three weeks, four months

Bodies entangled with no space to breathe
Her body unwrapped like green plantain
Too ripe for nature's permission.

Ship travelers
Bond over sorrow
Ship travelers
Bond over home

Chapter 3: Indenture
To serve and be unprotected

No gold. Just land and more work.
No hope. Just lost men, women and child

She labours for freedom that never comes
Remembering it's the same sun that beats her back
Like the new hands of a man across her face.

She cries for protection
None.
She cries for home
None.

Despite the circumstances that affected a generation of people, paths were forged for a different generation to thrive.

Chapter 4: Culture
Still, they rise

Coconut milk grated and squeezed

Cookup rice. *Metemgee. Gilbaka* Curry.

The women dance in homes filled with music
Secrets shared in the bottom house built on friendship
Cultures creating and blending anew.

Gold earrings
On her ears,
Gold bangles
Dangle on her wrist.

Chapter 5: Thrive
You are gold

Up in the sky, eyes wide shut
By choice now, a traveller in the sky.
I look to see how the wrinkles on her hand
Match the pain in her eyes
How her history is my history, and her history too.

My hands, her hands.
I think, she thinks.
We lock eyes
My gold, she thinks.

I feel I breathe, I see.

Mirror, mirror on the wall
We are gold, so stand up tall.

Chutkhan
Tiara Jade Chutkhan

I have always been envious of the people who can trace their family history for generations. The people whose family photos sit proudly on their mantels and cabinets, revealing the distinguished faces of great-grandparents who worked the land and raised large families doing great things. The great-uncles and aunts are family heros, pioneering in their fields and creating a legacy for the family name.

Sephia-stained, black and white photos are the subject of conversations during family gatherings and holidays in their ornate frames. The stories of those individuals are told amongst the adults who grin with a fondness at the faces they've known all their lives or perhaps met once or twice as a child. The stories are ingrained in the minds of teenagers who have been reminded since childhood not to forget those who paved the way for them to be in their current position. They are told with grandiose to the young ones, painting vivid pictures of a time long before they were born.

I have long envied these individuals because I understand what a privilege this is. I hadn't truly seen a photo of my great-grandparents until my early twenties, after my grandmother's passing, my dad's mom. When I first held those printed pictures, perfectly preserved under a plastic sheet in a worn album, I was in awe. I studied the brown faces of my great-grandparents; my great-grandfather's round nose, my great-grandmother's long face, and their stoic expressions. I held a moment in time captured decades before I was born in my hands. Seeing these photographs reminded me of another mystery that I had wondered about for years—who was the man whose last name I carried?

Chutkhan is the last name I carry. I've never met anyone who had the same name or even a version close to it. I had never met my dad's father or even seen a picture of him. I only knew the few stories that had been shared with me growing up. My grandfather would drink a lot, he was controlling, and in my grandmother's words, "He was crazy." She had been married to him no more than two years when she took my dad, only six months old, and returned to her parent's home. Within a few months, she arranged to come to Canada on her own, leaving my dad in the care of her parents. She would lay the necessary bricks to begin their life in Canada and send for him when the time was right.

Years passed and at five years old, my dad immigrated to Canada to join his mother and now step-father in his grandmother's company. My grandfather would call from time to time, asking to speak to his son. From what I know, the conversations were brief, often with him asking to be sponsored to come to Canada. This was where the trail went cold for me for many years. This man, my grandfather, was a faceless character in my family history. No photos hung proudly on the wall, no stories of the achievements that came with hard work under Guyana's hot sun, and no one to tell me to be proud of the name that I carried.

I was around 12 years old when I learned a new fact that would later provide the first pieces to the puzzle I was trying to solve. My grandfather remarried a few years after my grandmother left and had a second son. He had given his second son the exact same name as my dad. Two Adrian Devindra Chutkhan's existed in the world. I was curious that my dad had Googled this half-brother, found an email address, and reached out. No response ever came. It would be more than 10 years later before I finally decided to give it a try myself.

One of the most important things to me since going on the journey of educating myself on my culture and roots has been asking questions about my family history. Who were my great-grandparents? Who were their parents? Who made that initial journey from India to the Caribbean? I think all Indo-Caribbeans can relate to how difficult and lengthy of a process this can be. Much of this information has been lost to time or simply not passed down for reasons we may never know. I was able to get some information from my mom's parents and my grandma's siblings. I learned that one of my great-great-grandparents came from Uttar Pradesh that more than one had no last name, using their single name as the one they passed on to their children and a great-great-grandmother was mixed race, Indian, Indigenous and white. With all this new information, I felt even more strongly about trying to locate my grandfather.

In June 2021, I started with my dad's half-brother, where we had left off all those years ago. A quick Google search gave me all I needed to get in contact. My clammy fingers gripped my phone tight as I attempted to construct an email that was not too formal nor too relaxed. I read it over multiple times, changing words around and restructuring sentences. I feared sounding too demanding or plained out, scaring him from responding to me. The reality was that this man was a stranger and likely didn't know that I existed. He owed me nothing. I still had to take the chance, knowing that no stone should be left unturned in this situation.

I was startled when I received a response one afternoon, only a few days later, not from him, but from his mother. She confirmed that Adrian was indeed my grandfather's second son (not that I had any doubt) and that at 17 years old, she had married my grandfather. She told me about her experience during the marriage, which I immediately realized was a similar experience to my grandmother. My grandfather drank too much, didn't like to work, and couldn't provide for his family. She left him after about four years of marriage. I asked her if she knew why my grandfather chose to give his second child the same name as this always seemed so strange to me. She told me he never explained to her why, but she felt that he was hurt after losing my dad and was trying to replace the son he never got to know. She ended her email by letting me know that her son's birthday was coming up on June 15. My jaw dropped— it was the same as my dad's.

One of the first things I told her was that I had never seen a picture of my grandfather. Perhaps because she was willing to help, or maybe felt sorry for the young girl in search of her grandfather, she dug out an old photo and sent it to me. I have always been so drawn to old photos and many times in my childhood, I would sit for hours staring at old photo albums, admiring my family members at different ages. Now, I looked at the young face of my grandfather, no more than 30 at the time, standing beside his new wife, holding his new son. The resemblance to my dad was striking.

She and I exchanged a few more emails, her telling me about her life after she left my grandfather and a bit about his family, me telling her the little bits I had heard about him from my grandmother and dad. I was glad to hear my grandfather's mother, my great-grandmother, was still alive and that he had several siblings who were also alive and well. She hadn't heard about him or looked him up since the day she left. All she knew was that he was likely living in Suriname.

At this point, I had begun keeping a notebook with all the tidbits of information I had. This puzzle had been tucked away for decades, collecting dust out of sight and mind. I felt like I poured out the pieces, a few coming together to create an image, but many still missing, hidden in nooks and crannies. I questioned my motives multiple times. Why did I so badly want to locate a man that "Was not worth looking for," in the words of his ex-wife?

I reached out to my grandmother's younger sister, curious if she knew anything about my grandfather's family. She echoed what I had previously heard about his drinking habits and said she would ask their sister in Guyana if she could find a phone number for him or one of his family members. After speaking to my aunt, and my grandfather's ex-wife, I realized just how eager these women were to help and how quickly they would get on the phone with siblings, nieces or nephews to ask for these favours. It was no longer just me who was looking for my grandfather; I had a small team. My aunt got back to me within two days with the phone number of my grandfather's youngest sister. This sister lived with my great-grandmother and took care of her. She was just a Whatsapp message away.

I was hesitant to call or send a message and the phone number sat on my phone as the weeks passed. The thought of messaging this distant aunt made me anxious. These people, though family by blood, didn't know me.

Much like the other Adrian, they owed me nothing, and I couldn't rule out the possibility that they may not want to speak with me. I feared the idea of a message gone unread or a response saying, "Please do not contact me." I feared another dead end, another year, or perhaps a decade without answers.

***

One night in August, while scrolling through a Facebook group dedicated to sharing pieces of Guyana's history, I thought of searching for my last name in the group. I'd seen a few posts where people asked if anyone recognized the last name or a person's photo. Maybe I'd find a family member or someone who could possibly help me. My search turned up empty, but I got the bright idea to look up my last name in the main Facebook search. My dad and I were the first two to pop up, but a few individuals with our names were below. Chutkhan. One of the names I recognized was my grandfather's brother. It was jotted down in my notebook after my aunt had told me weeks before. As my grandmother would say, "A madness hit me," and I sent him a message detailing my search for my grandfather and asking if he knew where he was and had a phone number where I could reach him. He was also friends with two of the other Chutkhans I came across and I sent them messages as well, this time asking if they were related, in case we just happened to share a name and nothing more. I checked my phone after every buzz I heard that day.

A few days later, I received a response from the pretty woman I had messaged with the last name Chutkhan.

Yes, that's my dad's brother, she said. *He lives in Suriname.*

She said she didn't know much about her dad's family history, nor did she know her uncle had a son. I resisted the urge to mention he actually had two. Just like the other women I had spoken to, she was eager to help me and said she would reach out to her aunts and see who was in contact with my grandfather. We exchanged numbers and continued our conversation over Whatsapp. This cousin lived in Trinidad, and I learned that my grandfather had lived there for several years.

She asked me if I knew the history of our last name—I certainly didn't. She explained that it had been the last name of a female ancestor who had come to Guyana from India. The name had been recorded incorrectly and was actually pronounced *cha-owt-can*. Chutkhan was the spelling and pronunciation that the logger had interpreted. I wished that there was more to the story; the first name of this woman, where in India she came from, and what year she immigrated. Sadly that was all that had made it this far. I thanked my cousin for sharing the story with me, but it stuck in my head for days. How many of our last names had been changed and recorded incorrectly based on what British officials interpreted? I thought about how many Indo-Caribbeans must not know their true family name.

My cousin soon provided me with the phone number of her aunt in Guyana, the same aunt my grandmother's sister had given me the number for. To my surprise, she said the family was excited to hear from me and very glad that I tried to find them. They were waiting for my call. My nerves kicked in again, and though I promised to call them that week, months went by. I'd often look at the number saved on my phone and think about what I'd say and how the conversation would go. I attempted to call once and didn't get a hold of her aunt, my aunt. It wasn't until April 2022 that I finally attempted again to send a message, knowing I would never get my answers if I never asked.

As my cousin had told me more than once, my aunt was eager to hear from me. She responded fast, letting me know that she would call me that evening when she returned home. True to her word, she did. When the call came, I was on the phone with my grandmother (my mom's mom). I quickly told her I had to go and pulled my hair out of the messy bun I'd been sporting all day. Looking as presentable as possible, I accepted the call.

A small brown face looked back at me. Her short hair was styled the way most Guyanese women her age wear theirs. She wore thin glasses, and I could see big brown eyes behind them. She offered me a warm smile.

"Can you hear me? Can you see me?" She asked.

I couldn't help, but laugh at the way older people are when they use technology.

"Yes, yes, I can see you," I said.

She asked how I was while shifting the camera, so I could see the older woman sitting next to her.

"That is your great-grandmother. She's 94, you know. She'll be 95 next month."

My great-grandmother is a small woman with small eyes and deep mahogany skin like my aunt. Her hair was full and pulled back in a ponytail. She smiled at me and spoke a few words that I had trouble making out. It was a heart-warming moment nonetheless, our first time seeing each other.

Again the phone was passed, this time to another aunt.

"Your grandfather is living in Suriname. I live in Suriname too. I am on holiday right now, but I will make contact with him when I return home. I promise. He'll love to hear from you." she told me.

I thanked her multiple times. I chatted with the three women a little longer, telling them about my life in Canada, work, and family. In turn, they told me about their jobs, showed me their home, and told me how much they had liked my grandmother when decades ago she and my grandfather had been married. My aunt shared God's blessings with me before we ended the call, her sister promising again to get in contact with my grandfather when she returned home. I promised to stay in touch.

***

Two weeks after we initially spoke, my aunt called me saying that she'd returned home to Suriname and had gone to see my grandfather immediately after she'd left the airport.

"He's so excited to speak with you," she wrote.

But there was still one more obstacle preventing me from finally speaking to this man I had done all I could to track down.

"He doesn't have a video phone, only a regular phone. He also doesn't have wifi."

My aunt said my grandfather's wife (a surprise as I didn't know he'd married—again) had a nephew that visited often. He could use the internet on his phone and call whenever he and his wife visited.

"You both must be patient. It will all work out as it's supposed to," she said.

After all the people I had spoken to over the past year who had helped me in my search, what was one more? For 25 years, I had never seen this man, my grandfather, so what were a few more days? As my aunt told me to, I remained patient, keeping my phone ringer on and keeping an eye on my Whatsapp. Two days later, much sooner than I anticipated, I received the call.

"Hello," I said, smiling at the unfamiliar face.

This was clearly the nephew I'd been told would contact me. Straight faced, he said hello and passed the phone, staring back at me was the face of an older man, my grandfather.

"What is your title?" He asked, his face extra close to the screen.

I was confused as to what he was asking. "My title?"

"Yes, your title. You're Chutkhan, no?"

"Oh! Yes, that's me. I'm Adrian's daughter."

My grandfather wore thin frames that covered small hooded eyes like his younger sister. His face was clean-shaven, minus the thick mustache that rested on his upper lip. His head was covered with black hair that showed no signs of thinning, opposite from my father, who is bald. His skin was the same mahogany shade as his mother's. The first thing that stood out to me was his nose, large and round, the exact nose my dad has. For the first time, I saw the other half of my dad, the features of his face that didn't belong to my grandma. The blood that I also carried.

After the pleasantries, he asked about my dad, making no attempt to hide that he wanted to speak to his son.

"Your grandmother has siblings in Canada, no? You know it was me who was supposed to come to Canada with your father. Your grandmother took him and didn't let me see him."

He went on a tangent, telling me that he didn't understand why my dad hadn't spoken to him in 20 years.

"20 years, you know. I haven't heard from him; I haven't seen a penny from him. I would never ask. No, I would never ask, but I want to know why. I never did him anything wrong."

My grandfather said that he bore no ill will towards my grandmother and that he was now too old to travel and wouldn't ever come to Canada. He stressed yet again that he wanted to speak to my dad and understand what he had done wrong.

"Maybe you can ask him and he will tell you. Then the next time we talk, I can speak to him."

I nodded and agreed to ask my dad, already well aware he wouldn't be so willing to talk.

"Is there anything else you want to say?" My grandfather asked.

I told him that I was glad to have finally seen and spoken to him. We said our goodbyes and ended the call.

As requested, I told my dad that his father had asked for him and was far more interested in speaking to him than I was. Just as I'd predicted, he told me he wasn't interested in speaking to his father or having any relationship with him. After all, went his whole life without him.

"He owes me nothing and I owe him nothing," my dad said.

The few times my dad had spoken to his father throughout his life had never been pleasant. For that reason and more, he chose to stop accepting the phone calls altogether. After speaking to my grandfather, I had to sit with the lackluster feeling that remained in my chest for the days that followed. For most of my life, I had wondered about this man; for the past year, I had worked to find him like a detective looking for clues to an active case. The moment had come and gone and hadn't been special. It wasn't a dramatic moment like you see in the movies when long-lost family members finally reconnect with each other. My dad said that he might feel ready to have a conversation with his father one of these days, but it would be on his own terms; he was in no rush. I wasn't able to bring them together, nor myself and my grandfather, really. He had his own agenda, it seemed, and I was more, so just someone who could be helpful to it.

I have always been envious of the people who can trace their family history for generations. Their grandfathers were family leaders who taught them life lessons and told them stories that later shaped their adulthood. They would look up to these grandfathers and tell their children about them, assuming the duty to never let their legacy die.

I have wonderful parents, aunts and grandmothers who have done everything for me and whose lives I will always be proud of and whose legacies I will always share, but I have long envied those individuals because I have now realized that in that one respect, I may never be them.

A-Train seat for Christmas

Chelsea DeBarros

Growing up in the New York City borough of Queens, I relied on the MTA's subway and bus systems to get to school. Commuters would be so packed together in the morning rush hour that getting off the bus was harder than staying on it. Everyone, including myself, wanted the holy grail of seats: *the single seat*. With plenty of personal space and easy access to the back door exit, it was an ideal spot to sit. Looking back on the times I spent longing to get a single seat; I realized that for freedom seekers in history, getting a seat on any part of the bus or the train represented more than a resting place for their aching legs; it was a sign that they were not inferior and had no reason to be discriminated against.

In 1893, Indian lawyer and Brahmin Mohandas Gandhi were thrown off the "Whites-only" carriage in the Pietermaritzburg train station for not obeying the segregation rules in South Africa. Shocked by his treatment on the train, Gandhi used civil disobedience to protest against racial segregation and discrimination against Indians. In his non-violent movements, he boycotted British institutions and encouraged the purchase of Indian goods to advocate for the equal and fair treatment of Indians in South Africa. Being a leader that made drastic changes to social order meant Gandhi had to make sacrifices. In 1922, he was arrested by British officials for acts of sedition.

Standing in solidarity with Gandhi was Marcus Garvey, a Jamaican-born Black nationalist and a leader of the Pan-Africanism movement. In the first two decades of the twentieth century, Garvey advocated for Black people to unify, connect with each other, and return to their homeland in Africa. Once together, they could truly be free from white colonial rule. Garvey also encouraged economic self-sufficiency by promoting entrepreneurship and support for Black-owned businesses.

In addition to these global leaders fighting for racial justice was my nanny, May, a brave critical thinker from New Forest. The town was located in Guyana, a country in South America whose population includes descendants from India, Africa, China, Portugal, and local Indigenous tribes. Following the Dutch's arrival to Guyana in the 15th century, enslaved Africans were brought during the 17th century to work on the sugar plantations. In the 18th century, the British took over the rule from the Dutch and imported Indians, Chinese, and Portuguese as indentured laborers to replace the slavery system in Guyana. Although Guyana is racially diverse, it is an English-speaking country due to its remaining a British colony for over a hundred years. Having established informal segregation between the white British and persons of color in Guyana, the British empire determined the cultural infrastructure of Guyana, its social institutions, imports, and exports.

May came to experience segregation firsthand while living in Guyana under British rule. In 1947, she was a rambunctious nine-year-old of Indian ancestry. She had dark brown skin, thick black hair that was medium length with slight waves, and bushy eyebrows and arms. She stood at four feet tall, slender, with her collar bones sticking out. Her most glaring feature was her almond-shaped eyes, dark brown yet bright. From a young age, May found her strength in being independent. She woke up at 7 a.m. every day to make tea for herself, boil rice for lunch, and iron her white top and blue skirt uniform.

The school was one of May's favorite places because she consistently did well, especially in her arithmetic and English classes. Her teachers told her that she could be someone important one day if she kept up the good work. Her Uncle David and Aunt Rose, two middle-aged Hindu rice farmers with two older children of their own, recently adopted May. She wanted to do good for her new family and make them proud. May's mother and Uncle David were siblings, and they resembled each other. Uncle David was tall and slender, with a light brown skin tone, almond-shaped eyes, and black, thick wavy hair. Aunt Rose was a heavy-set Indo-Guyanese woman with a medium brown skin tone, pink-colored bow-arrowed lips, and long, silky, straight black hair that remained in a bun.

Uncle David and Aunt Rose took May in when she was five years old. That's when her mother, lacking medical care, died from complications during the birth of her second child. Two years later, May lost her father to heart failure due to severe complications from diabetes. Uncle David and Aunt Rose were well aware of the country folk superstition associated with being orphaned, namely that orphans do not make suitable marriage partners because they bring bad luck. So the couple passed May off as their biological daughter. They also wanted to instil in May the values of the Hindu religion to keep her grounded and a part of the community.

Although May practiced Hinduism at home, she attended a Christ-centred Anglican school because it was a British-controlled institution. Aunt Rose warned May not to share that she practiced Hinduism since it was not socially accepted by the British. She explained to May that the British would go into Indo-Guyanese villages and cut down *Jhandi* flags that were placed in front of homes after they completed their *puja* (worship ritual). The flag was set on a bamboo pole and stuck into the ground to symbolize good over evil. Due to the empire's goal to "Christianize" those of East Indian heritage, Hindus practiced their religion discreetly.

On a sunny afternoon during recess in school, May ran out into the schoolyard ready to play, but a gate separated the British children from the Guyanese children of colour. May's curiosity took hold of her as she approached the gate. Two white British girls were dressed in costly white tops and green chequered skirts on the other side. With her face and fingers pressed against the gate holes, May asked two girls on the other side, "Can I come and play with you?"

The children looked to their headmistress, hesitant to respond to May. The nervous headmistress got up from her chair, adjusted her black dress, puckered her rose-colored lips, and squinted her stark blue eyes.

"Girl, leave these children alone! Go on!" she yelled at May as the British children scurried away from the gate. All the children on May's side of the fence froze as they watched the ordeal.

Not knowing any better, May thought it was personal. Perhaps she couldn't play with the British children because she didn't have a mother or father. Maybe the headmistress knew her family was Hindu, so the girls could not play with her. May could look down and hope that the mean teacher would not strike her. After that day, no one at May's school questioned why the British children had different teachers, administrators, and classrooms and could not talk or play with the kids on the other side of the gate. They did not realize it, but they were experiencing segregation, both informal and deadly.

Aunt Rose and Uncle David always included May in their family affairs at home. For Christmas in 1947, Uncle David decided to take May along on his journey to Georgetown, the country's capital and largest city, where his eldest brother lived. David explained that Georgetown was bustling and well decorated for the holidays during Christmas time. May's eyes widened as he told her of Chinese food, ice cream, soda pop, sweets, and seasonal imported fruits and vegetables like apples, cabbage, and grapes. He described an abundance of shoppers buying everything from shoes to auto parts and how the Bourda Market was stocked to the brim with toys like it was Santa's workshop.

On the morning of their journey, Aunt Rose presented May with a new white and pink pleated dress which May changed into. After brushing and oiling May's hair, Rose parted it in the middle and into two plaits. May felt like a movie star. It was the first time she had ever dressed up for an occasion. Her outfit seemed tailored as it suited her so well.

May and Uncle David took the Torani Steam Passenger Ferry to Rossignol. The ferry sat at New Amsterdam, waiting to load on passengers as vendors sold small-scale items on the docks and workers loaded cargo onto the ship's second deck.

The white people who sat on the upper deck were allowed to board first when they finished. Then the rest of the people came aboard, but there were no seats, so they stood up on the second deck near the cargo. May quickly ran to a corner of the lower deck. She looked up into the shining sky and to the left of her view were British men and women sitting in seats on the ship's upper deck. Without hesitation and full of curiosity, May pushed her way through towards the stairs with the intent to sit in the seats and look at the view of the water and land from the upper deck. She was almost up the stairs when a security guard and Uncle David came walking her way.

"No, no, no. You can't go there; it's only for white people," the Afro-Guyanese guard told her as he held May by the hand and brought her back down the stairs.

"Only for white people?" May pondered. She never heard anyone say that out loud, and quite frankly, she didn't know how to perceive the comment. May frowned when she couldn't see what the others saw from the upper deck and went back to the corner of the ship.

Finally, the steamer docked and Uncle David and May made their way to the second part of their journey: the railway from Rossignol station to Georgetown. Along the route, May saw other commuters. The British men were nicely dressed in straight pants, dress shirts, and blazers with a bow-tie, a hat, and for some, a cane. The women accompanying them wore casual dresses, flat shoes, and sun hats.

Having never seen railway cars in her life, May was amazed at the big, long black train carts connected to one another and moving simultaneously. The train was loud, which made it more invigorating for May and reignited her excitement. Once on the end carriage, May let her eyes wander out the window at the villages as they passed through them. Some areas were filled with an abundance of land, crops, palm trees, roaming animals, small markets, and the backyards of homes. The ride was bumpy and tossed her around from side to side. Everyone held on tightly for balance because there were no seats. The pungent farm-like smell was especially challenging, with everyone packed so close together. May asked Uncle David if she could peep into the next carriage. He let her go.

Carefully watching her step after exiting and entering each carriage, May slowly opened the door to the first carriage and saw the British men and women sitting in their seats, conversing with one another. Then she spotted what she was looking for: an empty seat. She ran over, sat down, swung her legs back and forth, and held onto the seat as she looked outside the window and grinned.

A few moments later, a security guard came walking down the aisle.

"You cannot be here. Let's go back that way," the white British security guard said as he guided May back to the end carriage.

May wondered why she could not occupy a seat no one else had wanted. She grew furious and fed up as she stood next to her uncle, who was near the goats and sheep. First, May could not play with the British children in school because the headmistress segregated the British school children from the Guyanese children of color. Then, she could not go to the upper deck of the steamship because it was reserved for white passengers. Now she was being denied a seat in a carriage with empty seats and had to stand with farm animals instead.

With extraordinary clarity, May understood she was not the problem, but it was the informal segregation that she lived under. It was a discriminatory and oppressive system curated by the British, and it tried unsuccessfully to force her into thinking of herself as less than.

My nanny did not get a train seat for Christmas. Instead, she got a ticket to a revolutionary mindset: discrimination and segregation of groups is how the colonists remained in power and controlled society. The longer we support the effects of the British system that divided people, the system will continue to master us and hinder unity

Fernweh
Michelle DeFreitas

I opened my front door and stepped into the hallway. It's a hot day here in the city and it's not the regular type of heat either. It's the heat that is so strong you can hardly breathe because the air around you feels so thick and heavy. Thankfully, the sky is clear, and thankfully there's a cool breeze coming in from the South, providing some relief from the dense air and intense heat.

It doesn't help that the air conditioning in our apartment building is out of order, but it's not a surprise. Our building manager would do anything to cut corners and save a few bucks, even if it means letting the tenants in our building suffer for a while.

I head down the dimly lit hallway to the elevators. Today I'm going to visit my grandma and grandpa. They live just a couple of floors above me. In fact, they live so close I see them quite often. I truly enjoy spending my time with them both.

You see, my grandparents left their country in the 1980s. They left their lives back home in Guyana and came here to Canada. My fondest memories growing up include our family parties; we used to call them "Fam Jams." They were a couple of times a year when all my aunties, uncles, and cousins would get together. We would eat until our bellies were full, the adults would drink, and we would all dance and laugh so hard until our bellies hurt. Curry, roti, fried rice, cook-up, fried plantain, and black cake. It was all there. For dessert, we would have tennis rolls or pine tarts. The food was so good that as soon as you smelt it, you'd have an appetite all over again, even if you just ate.

I would hear stories about "Home" at these parties and get-togethers that would run late into the night, sometimes resulting in us sleeping on our aunty's living room floor; I would hear stories about "Home." I knew where I lived was considered home, but it never felt like it. Not like the home my loved ones so fondly spoke of. These stories that my aunties and uncles and my father would tell would leave them smiling and laughing. You could see it in their eyes. They loved the life they made for themselves here, but they loved their life back in Guyana. So much so that even after living here for the past twenty years, they still called Guyana their home.

Even though I've never been there, I consider Guyana home too. Something in my soul yearns for Guyana. At times, I even feel like I miss it. But how can a person miss somewhere and truly yearn for a place in which they've never even been?

There's a word for that feeling. *Fernweh*. It is defined as "A consuming longing to be somewhere you've never been; an aching to be in a distant and unknown land, an ambiguous yearning for anything, anywhere else, as anyone else." I've felt Fernweh for as long as I can remember, which is why I love being around my grandparents. I could listen to them talk all day about going back "Home".

I want to feel the sun, and the breeze, walk the roads my father walked, and walk the streets my grandparents met on. I want to eat fresh mango and guinep and relish the sweet flavour of sugarcane.

For now, home is here in the city. The sounds of sirens and TTC buses echoed in the street. Home is here in my grandma's apartment, where as soon as she opens the door, it smells like curry. Fresh and still sitting on the stove by the time I arrive.

I come here often and ask for stories like the hummingbird aching for nectar. I savour it and write it because our family history has been a victim of time for so long.

My grandma does not talk much about her early life. In fact, it used to upset her whenever an auntie or uncle asked her about it. Her secrets will remain with her, locked in her heart. I swear it feels like she's thrown away the key.

My grandma's parents died when she was young and her only brother died by his own hands a very long time ago, long before I came. Even long before some of my aunties came along. The record-keeping in Guyana is abysmal at best. They didn't care to remember us, or whatever was remembered was destroyed or lost. I would get green with envy whenever someone would mention a great-great-grandfather or mother.

How fortunate must one be to reach back through time and touch the ones who came before them? The ones whose blood runs through your veins. I've always wanted to remember them, to honour them, but I don't even have a name. The worst thing of all is that I may never will.

"Natasha! Yuh here just in time. Grandma made curry. Come, try it fuh meh. See if it needs a little bit of salt."

I am the official curry tester, both in my house and when I visit grandma's.

She takes the spoon from the pot of curry and slaps it in the palm of her hand. She then puts her palm to her mouth, careful that none falls onto the floor. She licks her lips, then passes me a spoon. Grandma is very particular about how I take curry out of the pot. She always makes sure no one accidentally double dips when taste testing, so she uses the pot spoon to pour some onto my "Taste-testing" spoon.

As usual, it's amazing. No more salt is necessary. I taste the array of flavours and they dance along with my tongue. *Geera*, *achar*, masala, turmeric. The beef is savoury, delicate, and rich in flavour.

"Come nuh. I guh heat up some roti fuh yuh. You go sit down and say hi to Grandpa," she uses her chin to point toward the living room.

"So, Grandma, I wanted to ask you a bit about back home today. I wanted to hear about how you and Grandpa met."

My grandparents have been together for 62 years. With 13 children and a ton of grandchildren later, I have never heard about how they met.

I have a boyfriend I love, and I think of him when I'm around my grandparents. I wonder if we'll be able to have 62 years together. But even then, I still don't think that'd be enough time.

We step into the living room, where my grandpa is fast asleep in his spot on the couch. His sudoku book rests on his chest as he sleeps. Grandpa fell asleep with his bowl on the living room table as a big fan of ramen noodles. The fans are blowing all around the apartment, providing little relief from the heat.

I sit down on the couch with curry in my lap. Grandma steps into the living room with a plate of hot roti and places it on the table in front of me. I can see the steam rising off it.

"Well, so Daddy and I met when I was 15," she says as she takes a seat next to me on the couch. She's wearing her silk nightie and her jet black hair is tied back. She only has a bit of grey, and her hair is still long and thick. Even in her older age, she still looks the same as twenty years ago.

"I just started working at a cook shop by myself," she continued. "I remember when the owner told me I got the job." He said I would be gettin' paid $1.40 a week. I said, "Whoopie, whoopie, I'm rich!" She tells me, all while giggling.

"Daddy, your grandpa, was walking home when I finished work," she explains as she fondly looks into the distance with a faint smile on her face. "I was on my way home, walking the other way and he turned around and we started talking. He walked me home that night. The day after, he came to visit me at work, and we talked again. He came again after that, every day for a week, just to talk to me at the cook shop. Yes, girl, I remember those days. Good, good days. Those days we didn't call them restaurants; we call them cook shops."

I look over to my grandpa, still peacefully sleeping. The sudoku book rises and falls on his chest with each breath as he sleeps.

"So if you could go back to those days, would you, Grandma?" I ask.

"Nuh man, yuh silly. They were good days. Good days, but I had many more good days after dem. We got married and had babies. I had thirteen babies, yuh know? We had good days after, Natasha. I love those days, but I love what came after too."

Good days, I thought.

I wondered if I was in the middle of making stories I'd hopefully be able to tell my grandchildren in the future.

My grandma was fearless. She wasn't afraid to love. She didn't need to be back home. It made me think of my life, my love. Unlike my grandma, who was free to love, I had to hide the love I had.

Being the eldest daughter in an immigrant household, it wasn't easy to forge relationships. Not easy as it was for Grandma. There's a pressure that accompanies packing up your life and moving to a new country. A pressure to succeed and be perfect. We walk on eggshells to not disappoint our loved ones. How could we let them down?

For us, our love has to be hidden and discreet. It must be "Meet me outside your class" or "Meet me at our spot." Our love lies to our parents and tells our friends to cover for us. Our love is sneaking around, trying not to get caught even though we aren't doing anything wrong. Our love is crying in our bedrooms; hearts are broken without being able to tell our parents because we know we went behind their backs. Our love is having to heal ourselves.

I had to be a good daughter.

Good daughters aren't allowed to have boyfriends or talk to boys. We are required to be home at a specific time. Less we are bombarded with questions. When we finally do go out, we must report to our parents who we are going out with, where we are going, and supply the phone number of every person in attendance. God forbid we show up home a minute later than anticipated.

No boys, but the day will come when we're asked why we don't have a boyfriend or aren't married.

Despite how different my grandma's life was compared to mine, we were equally as similar to each other as we were different. We loved. We yearned for a place far away from this tiny apartment in the middle of the city.

I think about Grandma's life back home.

The curry on my plate is almost done.

Grandma is in the kitchen making chai on the stove.

The noise from the buses echoes down the street.

The sirens are blazing.

It's hot and there's a cool breeze pouring into the windows.

I look over at my sleeping grandfather.

I smell curry and chai.

I think about my lover.

I think about it all and I can feel a warmth in the bottom of my belly, slowly seeping into my veins and enveloping my entire chest.

An explosion of warmth and love and deep appreciation.

I am a culmination of the past and present. A product of my ancestors.

This is my home.

I have the power to love freely. It was given to me by the matriarch herself.

I have the power.

On Family Heirlooms
Amanda Dejesus

There's always a grandfather clock.

You will always find one in the affluent homes of been-here-for-generations white people.

I didn't initially understand the mixture of sorrow and yearning I would feel when I entered their artfully furnished spaces. I knew I ached at something, but it wasn't envy directed at their being materially favored nor at the beauty of the pieces themselves. In fact, it was something decidedly immaterial, something that reverberated in the air not only amongst these things, but seemingly *from* them.

I didn't know then that I was feeling the patina of time—flavorful layers borne of something being carefully kept and stewarded for generations; storied objects imbued with power that reverberated with legacy and love. They had literally created an air of palpable rootedness and were a grounding presence and reminder of their owner's history, their 'right' to be here, a tangible stamp and yet a psychic shout of, *I've been here, I belong*. I was feeling the presence of their family heirlooms come to life in their home.

This is not at all to assert that all other immigrants *don't* have this—many have absolutely been able to lift pieces of their family history; flee with them in tow in even the direst, horrifying of circumstances. But more often than not, this was not the reality for Indo-Caribbeans. When I asked my pop what he brought with him to America, he said, "Nothing to bring. I owned nothing." His words vibrated through my bones all the way back to his ancestors on a ship on their way to Guyana.

I grew to understand what generational wealth meant and the complicated feelings it brings up for us. I know now what I was mourning, then—ancestors that were too busy surviving at the moment to nurture any sense of sentimentality towards the future.

As I began to curate and cultivate my own sense of home, both within the walls of our house and my spirit, I grappled with what it meant to create a space that would act both as nourishment for and a reflection of that spirit. What did honoring my Guyanese, American-born, Flatbush, Brooklyn-bred heritage look like in this space? What furnishings are just trappings of white people's shit? Conversely, which of those objects have genuinely become heirlooms for me? Where is it wrong to refer to certain things as 'belonging' to white people in the first place, as if we're not allowed to acquire, accumulate—to *have*—opulence and superfluity and more tangible tokens of wealth, *family history*, to pass down?

Where is Guyana in my home? Is it self-hating to not have more representation of that? What does that even mean or begin to *look* like (keeping the protective plastic covering on my couch?). What is actual self-hatred versus loving the items I have honestly gathered and ascribed meaning to along the way of my personal journey? Does it matter what that looks like so long as it resonates with true personal power and authenticity, and should it matter? And, as is safely applied to most things in life—who define any of this for myself and my own, but for *me*? What family heirlooms could we possibly have as reminders of the lives and capacity of those who came before us when all too often, it feels like the only things that made it through the generations to be passed down were tragedy and trauma?

What are *our* grandfather clocks?

I wanted to look deeper into our legacy. To start gathering the things we *did* have, including and beyond physical tokens, from their time to ours, would weave our story around us; connect our sorrows and strengths down the line, from Bihar to Brooklyn. To begin hand-picking things to not only layer our future's homes, but the way they live their everyday lives, so our descendants can start having symbols to serve as constant subconscious reminders, *sacred* reminders that our history left us spiritual wounds, yes, but, once alchemized spiritual *gold*. Reminders that they can, quite literally, surround themselves with.

So what have I come up with so far? Here are just a few:

There's the turmeric tea I learned to make from my mother that, though descended from the *Haldi doodh* of our Indian ancestors, is like our curries (and us), an amalgamation of things that become something entirely different and stands on its own —a rendition of 'theirs,' and yet something wholly and completely *ours*. I can feel my great-grandmother in the star anise and grated ginger, the silken, healing warmth of a powerful and beloved matriarch, of feminine strength in multitudes. It's no accident that I've found myself pressing a hot cup of it into the hands of women who have come to, whether knowingly or not, share a burden of pain; that female cousins and other women of my heart will ask for it by name. Every time I brew a pot, her presence rises along with the steam— a presence that can be passed down in every cup, as it was for me.

From scratch, I learned how to make butter from my cherished middle *mamoo*, my maternal uncle, an addict who looked like Jesus and often walked through life like him. He's the first place I really learned that in knowing the trenches of life intimately, you also learn to love others differently. He was far from perfect, but one of the things his life taught me is that holiness never is that it actually isn't supposed to be.

There's the found antique table that my big mamoo and his wife sweetly decided was for us upon seeing all the wood in our home. We picked the stain together, and he refinished it twice because he's a perfectionist. He inlaid the top with two coins from his battalion in the Navy. And it was done, just in time to be part of our wedding gift. It stands in our history as the first physical heirloom created and imbued specifically with the intention of love for us, and it breaks my heart open in joy every time I look at it.

There's one of my favorite pictures of my dad back home in Canal as a sinewy-and-sun-kissed teenage boy, all curly hair and long arms, cradling the faces of the calves he had helped drop that morning. A boy who, when he first came to this country a couple of years later, ran out from his apartment building into both the streets of Brooklyn in a thunderstorm, in his underwear, no less, to bathe joyfully in the rain—bringing a part of his old home into this new land and making them one, much to the comedic horror of my mother. There is such a purity, a tenderness that connects these things of his life, reminding me to always make time to be that part of my dad, to dance in the rain with that same innocent abandon, to hold new life in my hands, to appreciate, in so many ways that I am *here*.

There's the fascinating picture of my husband's grandfather and the jaguar he'd killed. Back then, the life of such a precious animal would be taken out of absolute necessity, most likely for the protection of livestock or children. In the somber set of his face, you could see the difference in life experience compared to someone photographed killing an animal for sport—the latter suggests a luxury of time, freedom of thought, and energy. Freedom to do *anything* that didn't have an underlying inclination towards survival.

A *jaguar*— and this wasn't any *Naked and Afraid,* where there's standby medical intervention on set, just in case. This means that our men were hunters that could go into the Amazon jungle and come out alive, not two generations back. How often do we really stop to marvel at this?

There's our crate of records; my father's intermingled with my father-in-law's, the former's *Sangaam, Prem Kahani* and *Bob Marley and the Wailers* leaning against the latter's *Queen's Greatest Hits Vol 2, The Wall* and *Zep IV*. Perhaps one of the most beloved of these is a vinyl of Christmas carols, where a sketchily-illustrated Jim Reeves looks like he's about to crawl out of a giant wreath on the cover, looking all types of pure *jumbie*, and in a plaid cardigan, no less.

I would run into the fire for that crate of records. It is evident in a box that I can't be made to fit into one. These songs are a thread that runs through and connects every part of my identity, my lineage, and speaks it in a language everyone understands—music.

Then there's perhaps the most important of what is left to us, found in an immigrant work ethic merged with the American hustle and the New

Yorker one. It is a unique combination of the headway our parents made and the hope that they carried, along with our understanding of how to navigate this country and culture differently for having been born here—something that has felt akin to picking up weapons off the floor of an unknown arena and learning to use them while you're already in the throes of battle. We've been bred on a foundation of immigrant values in such a way that whatever success we build will remember the taste of hardship on its tongue just enough and will keep us humble enough that we won't forget to use it for good. In remembering the sorrows that we have come from, those places in the bedrock of our lineage that have been carved open and gouged out, we are also primed for the living water of our joys to flow more thoroughly through us, as deep and wide and high as they can go. This culminates in an immense power—not an object, but a mentality and a gift for living one's life.

We've been compounding and connecting generations of wisdom in one lifetime. We are the curse breakers, the trailblazers of our lineages. So many of us work not just to produce greatness while in our own survival mode, but to bridge the gap between ancestral greatness and the wisdom in their wounds, to synch their healing with our healing; doing the work to re-route and re-root our legacy in the strength of theirs and ours becoming one thing.

We are the embodiment of this process; in this, we are living heirlooms, chalices of transformation, a treasure infinite in the vastness of its reach—and perhaps the greatest kind of generational wealth of all.

There's one last piece of this heirloom collection I want to share with you. Plot twist—it's the beautifully ornate grandfather clock my father-in-law gifted us, a tall, proud beauty made of solid tiger oak with delicate, filigree hands.

There's a painting on its face—an old ship at sea, heading to a new land.

Rub Dye Rani

Aaron Ishamel

As Rani watched her last *Maticoor* guests leaving the house that evening, she collapsed her practiced smile into exhaustion. Her mother's house hummed with relatives washing dishes, handling trash and organizing sleeping arrangements. Rani sat coated with turmeric dye under an old tank top and basketball shorts. As she perched on a living room chair like a glistening statue, her three sisters-in-law, her *bhoujis*, the 'core' of her Maticoor, were dutifully milling around the room.

Babita, Rani's eldest bhouji, was sliding a large coffee table across the room. Short and stocky, Babita was usually the one in the room to move anything over 20 lbs.

Shazana, who had just married Rani's second eldest brother, was as thin as a candle, her wick's end always burning behind her eyes. She was busily ensuring the white sheets were laid equidistant around the L-shaped sofa, where Rani would be sleeping this evening.

Tiffany, engaged with Rani's youngest brother, scrolled on her phone as she picked up the smallest of items, migrating them with indifference. Tiffany traced the outline of the glistening bride-to-be with a manicured finger from across the room.

"How long do you have to keep this on again?" she said, denoting Rani's current turmeric-yellow-on-hazelnut skin tone. "I can't take you seriously when you look like a Simpson, Ra-Ra."

Rani laughed. "Never been on this side of the turmeric before. I'm iffy on the rules myself."

"Don't listen to dat *rakshas* coconut," said Babita in annoyance as she shifted a la-z-boy to make more space. Her pudgy face swelled with emotion looking Rani up and down. "Yuh shine like Guyana gold! Robendra jaw gun' drop come tomorrow. Watch."

Rani thought of Robbie, her fiancé, for just one more day. They were each in their respective houses, each glazed with dye as a cultural rite of passage to matrimony. Rani felt cakey under the thick, chalky scent of turmeric. Would the scent still linger tomorrow? Or into her honeymoon?

Shazana seemed to read her mind, offering, "Some people wash it off right after, but traditionally," she said, squatting and tweaking final blanket positions by the millimeter, "The dye is left on till you get ready for the wedding."

"Eh, heh," agreed Babita. "Rani skin gon' need to scrub with lime tomorrow. Just like meh own wedding day. Yuh know, Rani, when I was a young ting--"

Rani mouthed 'save me' to her other bhoujis. Tiffany dutifully nodded and hoisted a plant pot behind Babita's head. Shazana calmly took the pot out of Tiffany's hands and rested it elsewhere.

Rani chuckled, returning her attention to Babita, who was explaining the auspicious details of her own Maticoor long ago. As eldest bhouji, Babita played a prominent role in advising and guiding Rani through the old-fashioned, often antiquated, Indo-Caribbean wedding traditions Babita took judiciously.

"Per tradition, five young unmarried girls rub dye pon you."

Rani extended her freakishly long, bronzed arms. "Done. We could've had five on each arm tonight."

"Any *odd* number would've been fine. I believe the girls are supposed to represent purity, I believe." inserted Shazana.

Tiffany snorted. Babita ignored her. "Exactly. But older married women get to rub dye pon you afterwards because we bestow abie blessing pon you like married women ourselves."

"Quite the blessing Babita," Rani shifted her jaw around, recalling vividly. "I can still feel your fingers scrubbing dye into my face like you were erasing all of my sins." Rani grabbed a tissue and began soothing sore areas.

"Yuh welcome. Now come," Babita prompted.

Rani rose from her chair, her lengthy frame towering over everyone. All three bhouji's eyes tilted upwards. Rani would often feel like a walking skyscraper, eliciting the same tilted head-gawking reactions tourists reserve for the Empire State Building. But her sisters-in-law were her ride-or-dies, their beautiful bhouji eyes filled with warmth and love.

In two long strides, she'd already reached her destination.

Before sitting, she crumpled the tissue and tossed it like a free throw at a wastebasket across the room. It came apart mid-air, fluttering to the carpet. She was about to fling her arms in annoyance, but instinctively kept them at bay. When excited, Rani had to watch her arm's length. Rani stewed her teeth and plopped onto her makeshift bed. When she was angry, she had to limit how she paced. Rani always felt like she was apologizing for moving like a tall person.

"You are so lucky. Robbie is legit a great guy," said Shazana.

I guess I am lucky? Thought Rani. Lucky that...he chose me? Because would he have imagined that he would have to literally look up to the love of his life for the rest of his life? Rani instinctively sank lower into the couch as her bhoujis kept chatting.

"If you and Robbie have children—if that's what you want, of course—they are going to be *so* tall and gorgeous! Walking runway models," said Tiffany.

Rani's smile dimmed on the small asterisk she always placed in her head. Robbie was 5'11", and she was 6'3". Numbers she constantly reminded herself of. They measured the one thing people literally calculate when they first see them together.

Rani's eyes found Tiffany's face again, whose manicured fingers were creeping closer to Rani's head.

In an instant, Babita leapt from across the room and slapped Tiffany's wandering hand.

"Ow! You psycho," Tiffany jumped back, her eyes searching for that plant pot again. "I was just *trying* to take a clump of turmeric left on Ra-Ra's forehead."

Babita put herself between Rani and Tiffany. "If anybody touch dis bride, *licks* guh share."

Rani felt for the clump and plucked it from a few strands of hair. It was solid enough between her fingers that she shot it towards the wastebasket like another free throw. She missed again, a sticky yellow smudge now hanging just above the molding. Rani, once again, stewed her teeth silently. The confrontation comedically fizzled and Babita's attention drifted to Rani once again.

"Eh gyal, yuh leave any dye for deh next *dulahin*?" Babita chuckled, denoting the sheer volume of turmeric needed to coat Rani's lengthy frame.

Rani feigned a toothless grin. People constantly made comments about her height. Sure, it was a harmless statement, but it was a statement about her body. It's not a compliment, so you can't say thank you, but it isn't a personal attack either. So what do you say?

Rani usually said nothing.

Tiffany lightly rubbed her wrist, her irritation subsiding. "So what else is this bride not allowed to do, Master of Maticoor?"

"She can't touch nobody and nothing," said Babita.

"She's touching the floor—and the couch," replied Tiffany.

"And her clothes, technically," Shazana pointed out.

Babita sighed deeply. "Ya'll some real *cunumunu* yuh know. This is all so nobody 'bad eye' she, yuh know? Like if someone Nah wan this marriage to go through?"

"Which makes *sense* since the bride or groom are supposed to be watched over and protected tonight," said Shazana, more towards Rani. "They can't leave the premises, just to be safe. And you do sleepwalk, so this is the appropriate sleeping situation."

"Well, not since I was a kid. Also, why didn't we simply have this slumber party in my room?" Rani asked.

"Yuh mudda dun want you staining her good sheets."

"Who died and made you in charge?" said Tiffany.

"Tradition," Shazana sighed, reminding the room of Babita's eldest bhouji status.

Babita bowed gallantly. "Exactly. Anodda ting. People are only supposed to approach you from the front. Only wan bhouji —*me* —is allowed behind yuh back. All through the night, you should be backing a wall, with protection from the Goddess Durga near you."

Rani took a moment before responding. "Thank you. I honestly didn't know all of that. In the rush of all the rituals, you just kind of, you know, do what you're told."

"Babita is pretty good at filling in the generational gaps," admitted Shazana.

"Exactly. We're here to mansplain for you," said Tiffany.

"Great. So what's with the 'bad eye' talk?" said Rani.

"Historically, it's just meant to protect the bride from anyone trying to kill her," said Shazana. "Over time, it was stretched to include staying inside to keep away said bad eye."

Babita agreed. "And you mustn't peep the *dulaha* or he *bhariaat*. Yuh wan fuh mek he miss you lil."

Rani nodded. She thought of Robbie again. Stripped down to his shorts, dyed up to his scalp. His cousins were probably making jokes, maybe even short jokes on account of herself. Jokes always had this nugget of truth; they found a way to plant a tiny seed inside you. This unsettled Rani.

"Just be glad our ancestors didn't get the idea to have rub dye be masala or curry powder," said Tiffany.

"I am glad. Turmeric has so many benefits," inserted Shazana. "It naturally cleanses the body and has anti-inflammatory properties. A great way for you to keep calm if you have wedding jitters."

"To warm any cold feet yuh may be having," said Babita. Rani instinctively tucked her feet between the cushions. She was aware they were the largest.

"Oh!" remembered Shazana. "We didn't even talk about the purification parts of the rub-dye ritual. So your energy—"

"Arrite arrite, enough with the history lessons. We are talking up a storm tonight. Mrs. Robendra-to-be needs her sleep. Come bhoujis, let's make up abie bed now."

The rest of the evening unfolded with little fanfare. Teeth were brushed, pajamas donned, farts heard and then denied outright. One by one, each woman in the living room fell asleep.

Rani was the last to close her eyes. Dark regions of her mind started to wake as she drifted off to sleep, the heaviness of her eyes giving way.

However, the darkness did not sleep.

It got up.

***

Rani awoke in the hallway upstairs. She froze, trying to remember how she got there. She felt heavy and disoriented. Bits and pieces came to her as she stood still in the unlit corridor, afraid to touch anything with her turmeric-laden hands. She vaguely recalled how it was hard to get up from the couch, almost like peeling herself off the sofa. Did she sleepwalk again?

She heard voices coming from an open window. It was late in the night, but a few family members were still in the backyard celebrating in their own way.

Rani saw her three brothers drinking and playing dominoes. They sat on high barstools, which appeared to function like ordinary chairs to them, their feet casually planted on the ground rather than dangling. Her brothers, all varying heights within an inch of each other, their faces a healthy mishmash of *Aji*, *Nana* and a random chatch up the family tree. As they sat right underneath their childhood basketball hoop, Rani fondly remembered being included as their reliable fourth for two-on-two basketball, a chaotic tangle of twiggy brown limbs as they lept for jump balls and rebounds over the years.

Another thought nestled in Rani's mind as she watched them. *I end up borrowing their jeans all the time. Their jeans don't exactly make me feel pretty, but they at least cover my ankles.*

Gazing at her brothers slapping down dominoes and laughing, a spat of jealousy flared inside Rani. *Boys are given more positive treatment than girls for being tall. Height is often considered a masculine trait.*

Rani's smile wilted as that last thought grew. Where was this coming from? She had never heard that particular voice in her mind before. She quickly tore herself from the window.

Careful not to touch the bannister, she found her way downstairs. The bottom of her feet felt odd. Each step was warm to the touch as if the turmeric itself created a barrier from her actually feeling the cold floor. She noted the weird sensation.

In the kitchen, aunties were left sipping tea and slipping gossip. One of them struggled to reach a dish up in the cupboard, acquiring a footstool shortly after.

When they ask me to get something up high, I'm the most desirable person because I'm tall. But when it comes to my dating life, I'm suddenly the least desirable person.

More thoughts permeated Rani's head as she looked on. *They are your family, but they'll gawk at you at your wedding. You know this. That's why they want to be invited. Who doesn't want to see a freak show?*

The voice kept piling on.

You're not graceful. Your body is too stretched out. So is your face. Has Robbie got a good look at it yet? Or has his neck been cramped from always looking up?

She shook her head violently. What was happening? Why was she such a Negative Nancy all of a sudden? She felt heavier and heavier, weighed down by the rush of words finding footholds in her thoughts.

Rani craned her neck towards the living room, where she could see three bhouji bumps curled up on the floor.

Ra-Ra. Tiffany's nickname for you because you're twice as big as any other girl she hung out with.

The voice grew louder.

They all married your brothers. They are doing this out of duty. They are not your friends.

No, thought Rani, answering back. You're wrong. They love me.

Robbie loves me.

Does he? What do you guys do for fun? Strolls in the park and walks on the beach where people can see your height difference? Or dinners, shows, Netflix and takeout where you are both sitting down, blissfully unaware of said difference?

Rani held her temples, trying to rationalize. He is going to be my husband. We're equals.

Oh yeah, sure. But only when you're eye to eye with him. Isn't that what equal means?

And you being taller, well, that's not helping anybody...

The voice kept unearthing old thoughts Rani kept buried deep in her mind.

When do people say there's the elephant in the room? It's usually a giraffe when it comes to me.

What would the sex look like, with you, they all would wonder?

I don't feel very feminine when forced to wear men's clothes.

I can't wear high heels like ever.

Fee-Fi-Fo-Fum.

With each jab, she twisted and turned until she lost her balance, falling onto a glass table. She crashed and realized: there was no crash. Just a soft strangeness as time seemed to stop around her. Her eyes widened, and her voice collapsed at the glowing realization inside her throat.

Rani appeared in the living room doorway, truth starting to fill her eyes. She made her way towards the lump on the couch. She didn't care to mind the sisters on the floor anymore. Her feet passed right through Shazana's legs, Tiffany's torso, and Babita's head.

She stopped at the lump on the couch. The truth was right there. That feeling of getting up off the couch, peeling herself off of it. She was actually peeling herself off of herself.

She was simply a shade of an original, a resemblance, a mere glistening apparition. She was this Rub-Dye Rani now, her entire being a thin shell of turmeric dye.

She loomed over the real Rani. Her negative energy was coagulating, making her sick. She wanted to rest, to go back on the couch and lay there peacefully. But looking down, she knew it was no longer an option. Rub-Dye Rani's toes began to wisp away like chalky dust. Her feet, legs and chest began to crack and loosen like sand, falling into quiet nothingness around the real Rani. In her final moments, she stroked the forehead of the real Rani and whispered in silent sobs, "You're going to be okay. You're going to be much better without me."

The touch on Rani's forehead left a warm sensation tingling all over. Rani's eyes snapped open. She sat up and took in the room. Everyone was still asleep. But someone else was here. She felt it. Someone was standing right next to her.

Shazana stirred, her eyes squinting at Rani's long frame upright on the sofa in the moonlight.

"Hey. Are you okay? What happened?" Shazana whispered. "Bad dream?" A tissue box appeared under Rani's nose. Rani dabbed her forehead from the sweat.

Rani took a long moment before replying. "Shaz, what was that thing you were saying earlier? About energy?"

"Energy?"

"Energy, purification...?"

"Oh yes!" Shanaza rose quietly, scooting over. "The application of the turmeric dye is to 'purify' the body. Clearing your spiritual health so you don't bring negative energy into the union."

Negative energy, Rani thought.

"Someone with bad feelings or jealousy can unintentionally transfer negative energy to you, so the 'no touching' is about maintaining your own spiritual and physical health."

Rani instinctively felt her forehead where someone, allegedly, had pantomimed a *tikka*. "This negative energy...instead of people giving that to me, can the turmeric bring that all out of me, from the *inside?*"

Shazana gave it some thought. "I mean, yeah, sure. It's flushing out any toxins you may have. And if you're not bringing negative energy into the union, then all those fears, anxieties, pent-up angst, all that rises to the surface and just, go elsewhere."

Rani nodded slowly. "I think it did."

"Huh?" Shazana stared at her as the moonlight hit Rani through the tilted blinds of the window. "You look... different."

"I feel different like this weight came off."

Rani felt a strange calm inside her. Whatever was deemed toxic within her was gone. She no longer had to carry that baggage with her and into her next chapter with Robbie.

A clean slate.

Rani's eyes welled up. "For the first time in a long time, I feel... genuinely happy. I love you, gals. And I can't wait to see Robbie tomorrow."

Shazana couldn't help herself and let out a squeal, clasping her hands together. "We love you too! We can't wait either!"

Two pillows from either direction found Shazana's face.

"Ayuh, two love up, Mattie? Hush up, Nah, man," said Babita in a vicious whisper.

"Ladies! Tomorrow, we have a long day," snapped Tiffany, cucumbers shifting in each eye socket. "If you don't want to look like a beast, then I suggest we get our beauty sleep."

Rani shook her head and laughed, everyone grumbling back into slumber.

The crumpled tissue still in her hand, Rani tossed it blindly towards the wastebasket. Her neck snapped as she realized it went in. She smirked at herself and laid back down.

Exhaustion collapsed and fell away as a genuine smile took form on Rani's turmeric-coated face.

Leelawattie

Joshua Timothy Jaipaul

For Guyana, my grandmother, myself, and everyone who struggles to
understand all that we are in a world that prefers to tell us all that we are not.
We all stand on the shoulders of our ancestors, whose contributions are seldom
acknowledged and appreciated. Thank you for always encouraging me to pray
not for lighter burdens, but for broader shoulders. I see you, and I love you.

How nature intended. There was a time when things only flowed the way
nature intended, so this phrase in itself is a new development. Juliet stood
overlooking the world-renowned Kaieteur Falls: the highest single-drop
waterfall at 741 feet. She had never seen this beauty in-person, despite having
lived in Guyana for some 40-odd years.

At the time of leaving, she did not imagine coming back for more
than a funeral. She was glad she did. The fertile soil between her toes was
comforting. She remembered how good it had been for her and her children.
She found a nice little spot to sit and enjoy her Ovaltine cookies as she took in
the scenery that could not be done justice with words. She reached into her

bag and twisted the cap off of her thermos.

"When in Rome!" she exclaimed to herself.

She was instantly filled with memories of her grandkids coming over on the weekend, fighting over how many scoops of Milo they could each have. It really is the simple things.

The group wandered around, snapping selfies they swore they'd revisit after they hit the 'post' button—we all know how that goes. Juliet, a woman of 82, still relied on her trusty flip phone, which remained in her pocket during the entire trek. What sense was there in being anywhere mentally other than right where you were physical? Her kids and grandkids had nagged her for years to upgrade to a phone that could at least receive photographs, but she held firm. Deep down, she knew it would be the end of the few in-person visits she still got from them. She firmly believed that life was to be experienced fully and was notorious for reminding everyone about the importance of valuing time. She would hammer this home by saying, "You won't pass this way again." She was never rich by anyone's standards; she was wealthy in life lessons and in all the ways that meant something to her. Wisdom made her a one-percenter.

She looked around. All of the faces were different shades than hers, with people of all backgrounds, shapes and sizes. She knew what people probably thought to themselves: how was she cleared to be here? However, she knew that this time, these thoughts were tied to her size and age (her travelling solo might have something to do with it, too) rather than her skin tone, gender and accent. She stood five feet tall at best, but she could hold her own. She had especially strong legs, more than likely from all those years of chasing behind everyone with a pot spoon. That straw broom also brought the heat, and the way she would wallop everyone made you think it was a *cutlass* she was swinging! Even if these were their actual thoughts, she had surely silenced any critics by this point.

The group had been on their adventure for nearly four days, having started out in Georgetown. It was about an eight-hour ride to Mahdia, where they disembarked and set out on a trek through the Amazon Rainforest, setting up tents and surviving the good old-fashioned way. After about three days, they reached the base of Kaieteur Falls. At the outset, the group was 10 members in size, plus the guide, who was a born and bred Guyanese man, just like the ones she remembered growing up around. His role was to lead them on a journey back to themselves by journeying with them to one of the most captivating sights their eyes could ever witness. A unique twist to this experience was (unless it was to clarify instructions), this was to serve as a silent excursion, where physically you had company, but mentally and emotionally, all you had was you. She had heard about silent retreats and how much good they could do for a person, so naturally, she got curious. Feeling like she might not be able to cross off every single bucket list item, she was thrilled to find this one-of-a-kind experience that seemed to accomplish so many at once.

It had excited Juliet to think about returning to her homeland as a visitor and experiencing it in an entirely new way. Juliet was no stranger to silence and having to walk a lonely path on a crowded street. However, this was a chance to change the narrative: she was *choosing* this rather than having it be her only option. The family had been unkind, distancing themselves from her at every opportunity because she had suffered from epilepsy as a child. The seizures would draw ridicule rather than empathy, and she was so 'othered' that the family never thought twice about taking food off of her counter while she worked endless hours to feed her five children. She *owed* it to them for embarrassing them. The seizures, which were not in her control, signalled to her family impending doom rooted in superstition. It was believed that children with deformities of any kind were a bad omen, so these children wouldn't have the luxury of a very long life. Growing up epileptic and a woman in Guyana, she summed up her experience: "My best advice was wrong." Regardless of everything, Juliet considered herself lucky. How could she not—she had just made it to the top of Kaieteur Falls!

The group was preparing a celebratory feast by picking and foraging from the Amazon Rainforest—the original Whole Foods. Even though participants were informed of this in advance, Juliet had packed a few items that she wanted to be part of this feast— she didn't want to leave it up to chance and risk these meaningful items being left out. She diced her potatoes, onions, tomatoes and carrots and fanned the aroma directly into her nostrils. This was a moment of pure bliss. Her fellow climbers couldn't hold back their confusion for long. They had to ask: "I know it's not usually one of the first things people say when speaking for the first time, but how come you brought these common items all the way here for this special meal? I mean, I would imagine we'd just make magic from what this beautiful land offers up to us." Juliet, a lover of conversation and opportunities for sharing, perked up even more.

She shared with her new community members that when she was brought to Guyana, the British were hellbent on stripping the inhabitants of their identity while making it known that they would also never be accepted as British. Among the many restrictions imposed on indentured labourers was that they could not grow these items. The interior of Guyana was known to produce the best-tasting potatoes, but the community could not harvest or eat them without fear of punishment. Instead, they were forced to consume imported produce, which arguably was meant to strip the people of their connection to their land. Returning with these items in hand to enjoy atop the pride of Guyana was her way of reconnecting with herself and the home she was strategically evicted from.

"But if they can't be grown here, and you brought those all the way from Canada, technically, aren't those still just imported products?" asked the daughter of one of the climbers.

Juliet always had an especially soft spot for children because they said what they meant confidently. She smiled before assuring the girl that she had met a gentleman near a farmer's boarding house who directed her to what she needed. He didn't even accept money. Her victory was a victory for all Guyanese people, which was payment enough.

The starter items that had been thrown into the pot quickly became the base for the best soup that had ever graced their lips. Soup seemed poetic; Juliet's mother had loved it, and so had she. Juliet's oldest grandson had also developed a love for preparing and eating soup— a family tradition. It wasn't long before everyone had huddled around Juliet, her pot spoon like a microphone that she used to project her voice into their souls and out into the Amazon Rainforest. This was the thing legends were made of and far different from anything Juliet thought she would ever experience. She let herself feel how full-circle this moment truly was.

The look of pure satisfaction emanated from the faces of each adventurer. What could be more perfect than that moment? Juliet noticed the tour guide being overcome by sleepiness, nearly dropping his unfinished bowl. She couldn't resist.

"Yuh eyes bigga than yuh belly!" Laughter erupted, and in an instant, the whole troupe felt like family.

Juliet nearly shed a tear because she could have had it if she had wanted more soup. She went inward and expressed gratitude because gone were the days of her having nothing more than what she could scrape from the sides of the pot to nourish her body for the gruelling challenge of being and staying alive.

She was shaken out of her daze by a high-pitched scream. Everyone looked around, thinking it might have been the call of an exotic animal. The scream came again, bringing everyone up onto their feet. They followed the sound and traced it to the place they feared it had come from—the bottom of the Falls. There seemed to be a group of young people in a panic. The sound of the water crashing made it impossible to hear what they were saying, but within moments, the climbers at the top had an idea of what they were up against. From 741 feet above the ground, they saw a stream of blood. Understanding how quickly this situation could become worse, action was needed.

The guide paced quickly, trying to develop a solution that would not jeopardize the safety of his climbers. As she had always done, Juliet sprang into action. She unzipped her backpack and did a quick inspection, asking everyone for first aid supplies and anything else she might need. She was confident in what she had, but it would be better to have more supplies if possible. She prepared the harness equipment and instructed her team to help her descend down to the screaming explorers. Juliet looked like she had done this a million times, but that wasn't it. She knew that she was both the oldest and lightest team member while also having the most mental strength and physical endurance. Years of carrying bags of eddoes for miles had strengthened her muscles. For periods of time, wearing riot gear for protection as if it were loungewear prepared her mind. She knew she had lived longer and experienced more than anyone in her company, so if this mission was to experience any loss, she was okay with it being her.

At what seemed to be record-setting speed, Juliet was, once again, at the bottom of Kaieteur Falls. She raced over to the group of explorers and tried to understand what had happened. They shared with her that they were British scouts who had been completing the same trek Juliet and her group had. They became separated from their leader, who was walking behind them. He had slipped on some rocks while they were making their way and began to seize. They attempted to swim toward him after he had fallen into the water, but the current had carried him away despite their best efforts. In the midst of that, all five of the travellers had sustained various injuries. Juliet knew that there was no time to waste, so she unzipped her bag and got to work. She had made her choice; she would attempt to aid them on her own and rely on the rest of the group's strength to pull the scouts up the falls more quickly than if she helped them down to assist her.

In a way that was equal parts nurse and loving grandmother, Juliet pulled out her latest word search book and handed it to one of the women who looked like she could use a distraction. She then handed her clear plastic container of tamarind balls to one man who shared that he was diabetic. The other man looked like he had some minor bruises and perhaps a broken leg, so Juliet bandaged him and knew that she would have to serve as a crutch. The second woman was having trouble breathing, so Juliet handed her a bottle of Vick's to help ease the congestion. The third woman said that she had fallen near a hive of wasps and began reaching for her EpiPen. She asked

Juliet to read the instructions, check the expiry date and administer it to her.

Juliet did as she was asked, but her mind went to a different time and space. She remembered coming home from church one Sunday to find all of her books in a burning pile, courtesy of her brother. It was wrong for women to read—how dare she try to improve herself and give society a reason to re-evaluate its perception of her. And now, her reading ability could mean life or death for another woman. At that moment, she had never been more proud of herself. Juliet read the instructions to the woman after confirming the medication hadn't expired. Then, the woman winced and turned away, anticipating the pain. But it never came.

Juliet then said, "My darling, this is the part of your story where you save yourself."

She handed her the Epipen, and after wiping one another's tears, the medicine began taking effect.

Juliet escorted the group to the point of ascension. The six of them paused for a moment, feeling a whirlwind of emotions, and the group thanked her for all she had done. She had acted selflessly and without a second thought. They asked her if she would take a photo with them, so they could remember their hero. Juliet must have looked frozen to them because she was filled with shock. She was used to being pushed out of pictures by people who knew her best, and here she was being welcomed into one as a superhero to what were once five British strangers

Juliet never made it back up the Falls. She had sustained her own set of injuries during her rescue mission and had given away all of her resources to the young travellers so that they could make it. She had also dislocated her shoulders after telling the group to climb up on them to prevent injuring themselves further on some jagged edges. She was at peace. She had made herself proud in her 82 years, and she was content knowing that she always operated out of love rather than seeking credit.

Knowing her final breaths were near, she felt something hit her stomach with force as she lay there. She looked down and found a single Victoria Amazonica. Puzzled as to where it came from, she squinted to see off into the distance. Her years of watching *Animal Planet* confirmed what had brought her this sweet offering: a Hoatzin, of course. She smiled and fumbled around for her identification and a marker. She wanted to be remembered for all of her, not some. Juliet is the name she had chosen for herself before coming to Canada. Since we ask that history be honoured as it actually occurred, she felt moved in her final moments. She wrote a slash before "Juliet" and wrote "Leelawatie."

She wondered if Canal #1 on the west bank of the Demerara River had changed much. She wondered if her mother would have been proud of her after she cleared so many hurdles rather than let them stand in her way. She laughed, knowing her time was near and having remembered the infamous saying on t-shirts around the globe: "When I die and Heaven doesn't want me, take me straight to Guyana!" She shed a tear because, for the first time, she knew that she was going to be wanted and accepted. She couldn't help, but think that Guyana, how nature intended, didn't really feel like a second place to Heaven.

Branches of the Same Tree
Jamie Langford

My mother likes to say that you have to know where you come from to know who you are and the strength you possess. "Never forget where you come from," she signs my birthday cards. My grandmother died before I was born, but my mother tells me that I am very organized, just as she was. That I run my household in a tight manner just as she did. That I comb my daughter's hair and tie it up precisely how my grandmother did. I love to hear my mother talk about her childhood. I love to just watch my mother speak in general. You are instantly drawn to her warmth if you ever meet my mother. She laughs a lot, and she enjoys conversation and people. My mother speaks in color. Can you imagine that? She is so articulate when she is describing something; she makes you visualize it. I once read an obituary she wrote, and it was so vivacious that it was radiating with electric love. Honestly, I don't think she can help it. I don't think she even realizes when she does this. Grenada, my mother's birthplace, is a paradise here on earth. The island is infused with color and warmth. Grenada has infused my mother; somehow, everything she says somehow includes Grenada.

As her daughter, I see in color. I do not have the ability like my mother to speak in color, to describe something so vividly you can imagine it—but I can see the colors. Grenada embedded something in my mother, and she passed it down to me. I have always loved to look at trees. When my husband and I first met, I am sure he thought it was odd when I asked him to look at a tree and tell me what he saw. Now, after a decade, he asks me this question during our neighborhood walks amongst the trees. I like to imagine everything the tree has seen in its age. I love to watch willow trees because they are calming. Sometimes, they remind me of Rastas. My grandfather was an agricultural farmer, and I remember watching him speak to some of the men who worked his land. One day, he was talking to a young man with long beautiful dreads. Both men were so calm and peaceful. I obviously cannot speak for an entire group of people, but I imagine that all Grenadians are peaceful people like willow trees.

What is your favorite thing about yourself? Do you love the tenacity for life that everyone says you inherited from your grandmother? Or your eyes that look just like your father's? Is it your ability to call a spade for what it is, just like your mother? My mother and I are nothing alike, but we are exactly alike. People will stop me in the middle of a sentence to exclaim, "You sound just like your mom!" I have been submerged in my mother's ideologies, drenched in her likeness. My uncle once laughed at my love for table runners and pointed out my mother's love for them too. Until he mentioned it, I hadn't thought about where my love for table runners came from. Later, I learned my grandmother used to keep beautiful table runners on my family's dining room table. I can easily define who I am; I just have to define my mother. But what made my mother? Has my family subconsciously continued beliefs and practices over generations that are now embedded in me? Where do these beliefs and practices come from? Who am I without these beliefs and practices?

My great grandparents migrated to Grenada from India. My mother identifies as Grenadian. She has no connection to our ancestral history, but we look 100 percent Indian. As a kid, people used to ask me if I was a "Red dot Indian." I spent a great deal of my youth trying to explain that my mother is Indian, but from Grenada. It is perplexing to try and explain this to people. My father is African American, whatever that is supposed to mean. To avoid giving the "Educational Narrative," I generally just refer to myself as Black. This has worked out fine for me, but now I am a mother myself. I wonder how distant Grenada and India will be from my children's lives.

When I read Dionne Brand's *In a Map to the Door of No Return*, I felt a horrible embarrassment about my ability to so easily dismiss my ancestry and assimilate. I cannot imagine how my ancestors passed through the door of no return, how they were able to survive, leaving everything they knew for a world they knew nothing about. Now, I am reduced to "Black" because I am too lazy, too unwilling, to explain the reality of migration. Maya Angelou said, "I come as one; I stand as ten thousand." As I navigate through the perils of life, I realize that my ancestors have been holding me up to my whole life. When I come before you, it's not just me; it is all of the women before me. In understanding this, my reality changed.

My intention in writing this was to honor my mother's ancestry, but my father, who is African American, said something to me I couldn't ignore. For the first time in decades, he is living by himself. He told me that being allowed to live in his own space was the happiest he had ever been in his life. When he said this, I felt something awful in my stomach because I could identify with the feeling. My father and I are not close, but I share this in common with him. I value my own space; I need my own space. I do not function well with people in my space. Being married with children can be extremely challenging. My husband has told me how much he has had to adapt to my needs and try to understand me.

My father has always been someone who needed space, and my father's father was the same way. He died alone while living by himself. For the three of us, it is as if our personal space is the only space where we have some kind of control in our lives. Our space is the only place for our peace. As loving as he is, my youngest son has already started to show signs I can recognize. He, too, feels the need to guard his own space. Has the trauma my father's ancestors experienced been manifested and passed down from generation to generation? Where does this unexplainable feeling my grandfather, father, myself, and my son all have to guard our personal space come from? Why do we feel it is the only thing we have control of, and so we have to protect it? I cannot imagine what my ancestors endured during slavery, but all humans desire to have control. Control of their lives, their destiny, their fate. Has this desire for control of something in our lives manifested from my ancestor's trauma from slavery, where they had no control over any aspect of their lives?

Now, I am left with a new set of questions. Along with our rich history, am I contributing to the cycle of passing down generational trauma from what my ancestors had to endure? How do I shift the narrative and make sure our family ancestry enriches my children? We are the guardians of our history and we have a responsibility to pass down our true generational wealth and knowledge of ourselves to the next generation. I have the responsibility and honor of passing all of the memories down to my children. Each generation is able to add their own memories own self-acquired knowledge to this knowledge bank. Leaves may blow from the tree, but they are still a part of the tree.

Sunday Afternoon Cookup
Nalini Mahadeo

She retreated to her favourite spot in the corner of their oversized sectional sofa in the living room of their oversized house. She sought comfort staring at the unnatural bleach-blond animated man on their oversized television who was trying to dislocate his jaw to accommodate an oversized hamburger. She would normally smirk at the ridiculous eating habits of this man like she did every Sunday, but struggled as the two oversized personalities who sat at her dining room table overshadowed her bubbly spirit. This wasn't the usual Sunday afternoon she loved—this time, the big pot of rice, peas, and meat slow-cooked in a savoury garlic and onion broth with fresh thyme and a host of other herbs couldn't console her shattered soul. Cookup was the Guyanese answer to Sunday comfort food, a way to fill up your belly, empty the fridge, and utilize every food group in one shot.

"But I de taught y'all was happy," the older man stated while rubbing his head with his right palm.

Her father had aged a few years within a few weeks. His thinning hair wasn't comically jet black for a man in his 60s and his lips seemed to have thinned out as well.

"So did I," the big burly one with the bloodshot eyes said.

"When I dey hear what she do, meh was vex-vex-vex like meh wan kill myself."

Asha did her trademark eye roll like she always did when her father made idiotic comments like that. The overdramatic emotions of her community never failed to amuse her. She chalked it up to decades of watching the unrealistic world of Bollywood cinema.

"Imagine how I felt! She is the love of my life and did *this* to me!" David's voice rose.

"I am so ashamed. Dis how she always behaves since she was small." Her dad took a long swig of his mixed Jack Daniels and Coke drink.

"I knew what she was like when we met and chose to overlook it." Asha's husband looked in her direction; his blue irises burned a hole in her forehead.

She shrunk to the size of their toddler as the men continued to discuss their anguish as if Asha wasn't in the room. Her mind flooded with flashbacks to the days prior when the burly one punched an oversized hole in the wall that separated the kitchen and living room; the drywall caved in as if a wrecking ball got to it. Asha considered reaching for the largest knife in the mahogany Cuisinart block just steps away if his rage continued. Her focus was on protecting their tear-streaked, red-faced two-year-old and her own face. He never laid a hand on her before, but the bull was teased enough that to be gored would mean she would fall in line with others before her and become another stereotypical statistic. Asha was very familiar with the treatment of the women in her community, though she never thought she would become one of them. After all, she broke the mould and married a white man who unknowingly introduced and kept a certain peace within the family. Her parents are no longer worried about Asha's dynamic and modern behaviour affecting their reputation within the community.

Her mind returned to the equally uncomfortable reality of their oversized sectional sofa, where Asha noticed her mother's similar body language on the other end. Kamla's voice cracked as she called for her two granddaughters' attention, offering them the freshly made cookup she prepared before they stormed the oversized house as they did every Sunday.

The sound of her heartbeat and blood coursing through her body flooded her ears. It was a welcome sound to drown out the character assassination unfolding at the oversized marble dining table, paired perfectly with studded linen chairs that she now hated.

"She doesn't have any male friends, so why him? What the fuck did he promise her?"

"You think a man like da has anything fuh promise? The new broom does sweep clean."

Like most West Indians, her father wasn't one to mince words. There was no shortage of metaphors to apply to any situation, especially ones of discomfort. He was typically a jolly old Guyanese soul, always ready to indulge in an alcoholic beverage and lime. Their voices became inaudible as she reminisced on the numerous hot meals they ate around the oversized table; the meals she forced herself to provide for her family almost daily, which included side dishes of constant critique and backhanded compliments from David. It dawned on Asha that besides the minimal dose of Guyanese heritage her parents injected into their oversized home each Sunday, the weekdays reflected little to no reference to her culture. David turned his nose up at the smell of curry and often described the other staple dishes as baby mush. Asha always bit her lips when her husband would seek validation for his masterful seasoning and grilling skills he learned from spending a lifetime in the restaurant scene due to his family's legacy. Although occasional, he made sure she took notice of his talent by leaving all the equipment and mess for her to clean. Besides Asha's love for *soca* and *chutney* music, their life did not appear as a blend of two very different cultures; rather, it resembled a modern European family in the perfect city to live their own cookup life in Toronto.

"I just don't know what went wrong...I have given her everything! I work so hard and still...this?"

It shook Asha to hear the rage and agitation return to David's demeanour. She could hear the alcohol reaching its limit as he had a light tolerance for a man of his stature.

"Ungrateful! I nevah think she woulda do dis. And wit who! I feel sorry fuh dem two little angels. I don't know why God had to punish *me* like dis!"

He poured himself another drink to distract from the tears filling his yellowed eyes. He silently signalled to Kamla for more ice. She desperately wanted someone to lift the lid on the belittlement just like they do with the simmering pot, but it was doubtful the focus would be redirected to what the real issue was.

"The girls will be fine. I will tell you one thing, though, I will never trust her again. I don't know if I could get past this."

Asha's eyes widened at the remark her husband made. Her fingers crept slowly to reach for her cell phone, ready to expose the sea of text messages from the Burly Blue Eyes' coworker around the time she was still recovering from her first childbirth. She never had solid evidence, but the text conversations she forwarded to herself, along with the unusual secrecy, bizarre late-night uniform wash, and mysterious disappearance, told her all she needed to know. She shrunk further into the oversized couch and pulled the fur throw up to her chest, replaying when they lay naked in their oversized matrimonial bed and he couldn't climax, declaring her intimate parts felt like a bowling alley. Although he quickly back-peddled in an attempt to save his physical shame, his words already poisoned her mind and heart. Even when confronted with all the evidence, David managed to flip the script and make himself out to be the victim. Denial was at the forefront, but he made a valiant effort and convinced Asha it was all in her head. He covertly blamed her for being more affectionate to their new baby and none of it was directed at him. A wave of nausea took control of her body and washed away her ambition for a revenge smear campaign.

"Mama, pooh-pooh!" their youngest announced, jolting Asha back to reality.

Mya cocked her head to the side to match her mother's and buried her face into her chest. Asha mustered up the energy to make it off the oversized couch and climb the grand staircase lined with framed memories of smiling faces with Mya leading the way for a diaper change. Her father and husband continued to clink glasses and devour the cucumber with salt and pepper sauce. Neither of the men acknowledged Asha, her mom, or the two little girls as they floated past them.

Asha stretched out the time away from the oversized sectional with multiple rounds of peekaboo and tickles. Every effort was made on her part to ensure their daughters were oblivious to the thick tension in the oversized house, despite the oversized hole that separated the kitchen and living room. It was also to avoid the long-term psychological effects of watching their parents put the two of them in the middle of their marriage. The girls' infectious laughter filled the air and for a brief moment, Asha felt some strength return to her limp body. Celine and Mya were the two picture-perfect blends of cross-culture. Celine with her creamy caramel skin, the olive undertones from her Mediterranean paternal side, and big round dark eyes like her Indo-Guyanese mother. Mya, with her brunette curls highlighted with bronze pieces and her deceivingly shy smile she inherited from Asha.

David always had a sore spot; neither child was blessed with his perfect blue eyes. He pointed it out occasionally, which triggered the painful moment when she announced her pregnancy with Mya. His initial reaction was to inquire who else she spent time with. It was a low blow when he probed about Mya's paternity again when he found out what she did and an even lower blow when he gossiped about it to her parents and anyone who would listen. The slander wasn't expected, but it wasn't surprising either. The threat of a DNA test slammed Asha into another level of hurt. David was a master of creating a narrative and image that would have everyone swoon over his personality. His larger-than-life charisma, body paired with blue eyes, and his never-ending anecdotes and critique of others disguised as jokes always resonated with people long after they left his presence.

Her body weakened again, making her feel like she was the meat in the cookup at the bottom of the well-aged pot being stirred to the top and back down to cook closer to the heat.

She removed herself from the girls as her mother decided to braid their hair and sought isolation in her recently renovated ensuite washroom. A hysterical laugh emerged from her pale face as she walked past his and her closets in their master bedroom. Kamla stormed in and quickly halted her daughter's laugh with a stare. Her scowl immediately returned to her droopy face.

"Gyal! Behave yourself before dem two get more vex! Me ain't know how much langa yuh faddah ah guh punish me fuh yuh schupidness. Me jus cyan undastand wha jumbie tek yuh mind. Meh guh, call de *pandit* Aunty Baby does see fuh *jharay* you, dem pickney, and dis house. Some real blessings guh mek dis house nice again. Abey cyan live like dis none more."

She pretended to ignore her mother, even though her words always dug a knife into her heart. Since she was a teenager, Asha and Kamla had a strained relationship. It often had to do with Asha's constant need for attention, and affection, especially her crusade to be the contemporary Canadian woman she was literally born to be. The complexity of self-sacrifice and the inability to create and maintain happiness unattached to a male never sat well with Asha. Even though Kamla never agreed or gave her blessing to David and Asha's union, her attitude softened with Celine's arrival.

Asha tilted her head to the right and ran her hands across the clothes hanging in her closet. David finally gave her the walk-in closet he had continuously promised eight years ago when he initially shared his oversized vision for their oversized home. Only this promise was fulfilled because the doors met the same fate as the wall between the kitchen and living room; they were removed as they were just another casualty of his temper.

She stood at the top of the stairs for a brief moment, smiled at the faces beaming back at her from the oversized Ikea frames and descended to the oversized living room.

"Eh!" Asha was finally acknowledged by a male in the house. "Tek out some cookup fuh David while it still hawt."

"No, it's ok, Deo. I can get it myself. I'm used to doing *everything* myself around here," Burly Blue Eyes stated matter of factly.

Her small shoulders curled in once again as she retreated to the corner of their oversized sectional sofa and waited in vain for this Sunday to end

Two Times Rejected
Jaimini Mangrue

Growing up as a young Guyanese girl in Scarborough, Ontario, during the '90s was an experience.

I went to a tiny 600-student school in the burbs of Toronto. Today, Scarborough is the epitome of multiculturalism, where the vast majority of citizens are recent immigrants. However, back in the '90s, people of color were few and far between.

We (immigrants and the children of immigrants) lived in the city's cheapest, most rundown apartment buildings, which were a 45-minute bus ride from school. As a child, I associated living in a house with being white. The white kids were the ones that lived in the houses so close to the school that they got to walk. The rest of us were envious because this meant they did not need to wake up at the crack of dawn (or so it felt, as a child) to catch the bus. Our mom would abruptly shake my brother awake and me at 6 a.m. to the same instructions every morning: "Go brush yuh *teet*, bade, and wipe out the *booboo* pon yuh eye." This whole operation needed to be done in 15 minutes before we got my mom's favourite saying: "Aiyodis slow like-ah moomoo goat." After we showered, my mom would comb our hair, making sure to rub in enough oil to fry an aloo ball. She would then plait mine into two long pigtails down my back. After eating, she would hand us our lunches and send us off to school on the bus.

Of the 600 kids in that school, only about 10% of us were people of colour. As a child, you don't really notice that kind of thing until it is blatantly pointed out to you.

AT BEST, the POC kids at school were disregarded and mercilessly bullied at worst. It felt as if just daring to exist in a different skin tone was the biggest offence to the dominant group of students. I distinctly remember the first time I was called "Paki." I had just been passing by a group of older students after getting off the bus when the word was jeered at me in disgust. It immediately filled my little four-year-old heart with confusion and fear. I didn't understand what the word "Paki" meant, but I knew it was bad. Instances of this went on for the next near-decade or so of my life, with me experiencing the same emotional response to the word each time. The way these kids said the word with so much disdain made it clear to me that they felt I was a lesser person just for having brown skin.

Later, I learned that the word was a derogatory shortening of "Pakistani" and was used as an insult against anyone of South Asian descent. This made no sense to me. Why would a country, culture, or identity be used as an insult?

Anything that was not part of the dominant "Canadian" culture was ridiculed. This meant that a lot of kids were left in a constant state of preoccupation with trying to fit in—some even rubbing baby powder on their skin to appear lighter. I remember bringing *channa* for lunch one day and being so excited to dig in. That is until one kid yelled, "Why does your food look like animal droppings?" while making a face like he was ready to retch his dry white-bread bologna sandwich all over his desk. Nothing has made me lose my appetite that fast ever since. That same afternoon I asked my mom to start packing me sandwiches every day instead. Being the no-nonsense Guyanese mother she was, she refused to give in to *eye-pass*. After she let out a few distinctly Guyanese expletives that would have earned my siblings and me an early spot in a grave if we dared to repeat them, my mom made it her mission to instil in us that same confidence she had in all that she was, and all that she came from. My parents' stubbornness to conform demonstrated that we didn't need validation from others to exist as we were.

Still, the struggle continued. Years later, I came to understand that at the time, people of colour in the community I grew up in did not have separate cultural identities. Not under the Eurocentric society of elementary-aged kids and their parents, anyways. If you weren't 89.8% British, 10% Irish and 0.2% French, you were shoved haphazardly into skin-coloured boxes labelled "Indian," "Black," and "Chinese," crushing all the nuances of our different cultures and diasporic upbringings brought to our identities. Individuality did not exist for a person of colour— you were simply whatever category the non-POC population decided you fell into.

Eventually, I moved to Brampton, Ontario. Brampton is known for its thriving community of people of colour—the most predominant group being South Asian immigrants and children of immigrants. Brampton is a community of diversity in the greatest sense of the word. It's a place where diversity goes beyond just having a few token representatives of various skin colours at the bottom of the pyramid. Instead, people of colour have more opportunities to occupy all spaces and different cultures and customs are expressed in their most authentic state.

Coming from a place where racial aggressions were the norm, you can imagine my shock and relief at walking into a school where the majority of people looked somewhat like me. On my first day, I felt that I would finally be accepted since we were all some shade of brown. After all, we were the same, right? It didn't matter what country we were from—brown is brown. That's what I had been forced to believe for so many years anyways.

It turned out I was very, very wrong.

I realised really fast that to some of my South Asian peers (more specifically, some of my Indian peers), we were not the same. Coolie people were *beneath* them.

Honestly, the rejection and dismissal from fellow people of colour stung more than when it came from white people. Growing up, elders in the Guyanese community often talked of white people as the "Other." At the time, I just believed we were fundamentally different groups and that nothing could help that. Whenever I experienced confusion over racist behaviours and microaggressions, I'd remember my *ajee* or random *chach's* saying, "Well, white people do stay like dah." It became a phrase that became a common saying because they had faced the same prejudice before me. It was prejudice that was passed down through generations.

So when they made fun of my food, baulked at my brown skin, called me "Curry" and "Paki," or excluded me from their social circle, I expected this behaviour. I had a good group of multicultural friends who all had similar experiences from time to time. The disrespect had become normalised—not that we accepted it. We could argue back all we wanted, but at the end of the day, we were in a "White man country," as our elders had been (wrongly) told and were now telling us. This treatment was nothing new.

When it came to facing disdain from people with whom you stood in solidarity against shared prejudice, the rejection was even more disappointing.

Eventually, I gained a better understanding of Guyanese history and where we came from. I knew my ancestors had Indian roots and that at one point in the past, I may have been kin to the same people who were now telling me that "Caribbean people have no culture" or that "Coolie people are low caste." They did not want to be associated with people they regarded as their antithesis.

This was quite the shock to a person who grew up being in awe that, in some distant way, the strands of our DNA had been cut from the same cloth. Still, although we all knew that Indians and Indo-Caribbeans had once felt the same soil beneath their feet, centuries had placed too much distance between us. An ocean had made us (Indo-Caribbeans) unfamiliar and wild territory.

I remember being told that I'm not really "Brown" (used as a synonym for South Asian/Indian). Like many of my fellow Indo-Caribbean peers had been told before, I was informed that our history was too disgraceful, our way of life too tainted, and our bloodline too murky to be "Brown." The indentureship we were born out of was akin to slavery and was something only people of low intellect and status would fall prey to. People who were *Coolie*.

I did not want to be considered Indian. To me, that ship had sailed in 1838 when the *Whitby* left the ports of Calcutta. I wanted my community not to be disrespected simply because we weren't Indian. I did not want to be considered a watered-down version of what could have been had my ancestors not crossed the Atlantic Ocean. My Indo-Caribbean identity deserved to be recognized as fully and completely as any other identity. As much as we have retained our ancestors' Indian ways and customs, our history has forced us to become nuanced. Like others, we have our own unique diasporic experience and have gained our own vibrant culture. A culture forged by the trauma of indentureship, the resilience of the oppressed, and the opportunity to learn from and coexist with so many other nations who we joined across an ocean to become one people. We are not watered down; we are everything we've ever been, everything we've come to be, and everything we've passed through.

Until the point when my cultural identity was being quantified and qualified by people who felt the need to evaluate brownness, the word "Coolie" was a proud identifier to me. But suddenly, in the mouth of people who spat it at me with ridicule, it was no longer a word I wanted to describe myself as when speaking to those outside of the Caribbean community. Not when the word seemed to harbour so many insulting stereotypes against Caribbean people.

Like many others, I learned of these stereotypes through seemingly well-meaning conversations and frustrating life experiences. Life experiences like those of multiple friends and family members who were left heartbroken and insulted when their relationships with long-term *desi* partners abruptly ended so that these partners could find someone more acceptable from their own cultures instead. They made it clear that a Coolie partner was not marriage material. Coolie people fit into the rebellious, careless phase of their life plan, but could not possibly be respectable, serious life partners.

Another friend was devastated when she tried out for her university's South Asian dance team and was immediately rejected by the group despite having almost two decades of experience in Indian classical dance. They felt that since her ancestors had left India and did not speak any Indian languages, she could not possibly represent the Indian diaspora (the irony). She was told that she was not welcome as a person who was not Indian and that she should stick to her own.

Through tears, she asked her mom why she had painstakingly trained in classical Indian dance her whole life, only to be rejected because she was Coolie. The dance that her parents nostalgically clung to as a memory of home was one she suddenly had no claim to. In the eyes of her peers, this dance was not really hers, or any other Coolie person's, to perform regardless of the historical ties we had to it.

In high school, a South Asian acquaintance shamelessly told me that he'd love to date a Guyanese girl solely because "Coolie girls were easy." Later on in life, I was shocked when a close friend thought she was complimenting me by saying, "My mom would like you because you're not wild or slutty like other Guyanese girls." Another insisted that West Indian chutney defiled Indian music, which was pure and thoughtful, and instead made it a joke.

In those moments, I would think of my mom, the most pure-hearted and innocent woman I know; who loves to sing *bhajans* and lead *chowtals*, plays harmonium, grows the greenest garden, runs a business with my dad and who is talented in so many other ways. She is unconditionally caring, infinitely supportive, and courageously unshakeable during tough times. I can't believe that someone could describe the identity of a person like her, a kind and resilient Guyanese woman who's thrived despite the weight of intergenerational burdens in such disparaging ways.

I also think of my dad. My dad, a business owner and an accomplished martial artist, is the epitome of confidence and self-discipline. His outlook on life is one of optimism and always doing good for others. Like many Guyanese dads, mine can find humour and a life lesson in every situation. He grew up so poor that my resourceful and hardworking *ajee* could often only put together a meal of *marr* and rice for him and his siblings. He was eventually forced to leave school early in favour of being able to provide for his family. He faced countless tragedies and losses at a young age yet made a life for himself in a country that did not want to see people like him succeed.

My parents made sure my siblings and I got to experience more than they could even dream of growing up in Guyana. So many people of colour share a similar experience, yet there is a divide in who is respected for it and who is not.

These comments always made me wonder why Indo-Caribbean culture was held in such low regard, especially by those we stemmed from. Why were there constant attempts to use our identity as an insult? Why were Indo-Caribbean struggles synonymous with being inferior? Did they not understand that our histories are inherently intertwined and that our cultures branch off a common thread? That our DNA *is* a common thread? I've since realised that I was not the only one asking these questions.

Gaiutra Bahadur's book *Coolie Woman* explained how Indo-Caribbeans faced the same racist aggressions as Indians did from white New Yorkers who grouped all brown-skinned people in the same category. However, despite this shared suffering, Indo-Caribbeans were still othered by the Indian community and were never seen as equals. The book also recalled how Coolies who returned to India after servitude (a task the British made near impossible) were often no longer welcome in the villages they came from. They no longer fit into the community that many Coolies had sacrificed years of their lives for in the blind hope that they would return to their country better off than before.

This rejection has rippled through time and is echoed generations later in those of us who are both two times removed and two times rejected. I am hopeful that perhaps the waves of rejection that once came crashing down on eager open hearts are now more like weak tides that creep in lower and less often with time as Caribbean identities become more understood.

Despite my experiences, I enjoyed my school days and looked back on the memories very fondly. I've also been blessed to have many great South Asian friends who have made me feel valued and respected throughout my life. It would be unfair and inaccurate of me to paint a whole community with such a narrow brush, especially one that I find so much comfort and familiarity in.

Maybe as a result of becoming older and more reflective, I'm able to see the compounded instances of racism and prejudice I experienced growing up as something more than just a few *botheration* people I had the misfortune of meeting. These experiences reflect something more long-standing and systematic. Indo-Caribbean prejudice is harmful to a community that has already faced centuries of rejection from both the white majority and the Indian community we branched off from. We do not deserve to be treated as if we are inferior for things outside of our control. The culture and identity honed by lifetimes of hardships are one we should be able to be proud of without scrutiny.

Time has taught me that colonialism thrived through pitting minority groups against each other and that it may be at the root of the rejection we all face from time to time. These kinds of prejudices can be unlearned. A lot of us become better people as we go through life and become aware of our shortcomings. I've been able to see people in my own life work to acknowledge and unlearn their biases.

The Indo-Caribbean story is one of resilience against all odds. Our history began in a place of violence and manipulation; however, there were many compounding reasons on top of this for why our ancestors left their homeland. Whether it was because they were falsely promised a better life or were fleeing from unfair treatment forced upon them by social constructs at the time, I like to think that they all shared a common quality: they were risk-takers.

Like their great-great-grandparents before them, my parents and likely your parents crossed an ocean with nothing, but the courage in their veins and the stubbornness to not shrink into a mold and accept the fate laid out for them. They took a chance because that chance was all they had. Whether they were accepted or not, they bulldozed on.

If you ever feel belittled for just existing, I want you to know:

You were meant for more than this. The same courage that flowed in the veins of those who came before you also flows in you. With that, you can cross any ocean that you may come to. Caribbean stubbornness is a force to be reckoned with.

Life Doesn't Stop
Alyssa Mongroo

On November 11, 2020, I woke up to a normal morning in my Boston apartment. I had just made breakfast, reviewed my notes for my Evidence class later that morning, and gone to shower. I was on call for class that day and my biggest worry was making sure that I didn't sound like an idiot in front of the class. It's funny, Evidence was my favourite class that semester, but like all law school classes, you can't help, but get nervous when you talk in front of the class—even when it's online.

After I showered, I got dressed in my newest set of lazy clothes. Zoom School of Law meant I didn't have to dress up or do my makeup. Even though I had to turn my camera on to talk in front of the class, I really couldn't have cared less about my appearance that day. I just wanted to get this cold call over with; what I thought would be my biggest worry that day. I got my computer setup, my phone propped up on my Amazon phone stand, and I logged into class.

Ten minutes into the lesson, I got a video call from a cousin in Trinidad that I hadn't spoken to in years. I figured he was probably just calling because he was bored or something, so I canceled the call. My phone continued to ring, so I canceled. Repeat. I started to think, "Something isn't right." My phone rang again. I answered.

"Alyssa, something happened to your grandmother."

"What?" I said calmly.

"You need to get your dad and tell him.... someone killed your grandmother."

"No. You're lying. She's fine. He would have called me and told me something like that happened."

I was convinced my cousin was trying to play some trick on me. I hung up and hesitantly called my dad. It was the first morning; he hadn't called his mom yet. He was just about to phone her when I did. That's when things began to spin.

About an hour after we found out, images of crime scene tape across my grandparent's house hit Trinidadian news stations. Media outlets were posting my grandmother's photos on Facebook, some with photos that none of my family ever had. *Mother found dead* and *Grandma strangled to death* were the headlines. It was utterly heartbreaking. My phone would not stop ringing with texts and Whatsapp messages from people I barely knew, people who didn't talk to my grandma or us. I knew they meant well, and I was trying to be nice, but I wanted it to stop.

I went home to New York the next day to stay with my brother while my parents went to Trinidad for the funeral. He's old enough to stay by himself, but I didn't want him to be alone and I didn't want to be alone. I've always had a fear of funerals, and my grandma knew this. When I was 12, a distant family member passed away and my parents took my brother and me to the funeral despite my grandma telling them not to. She knew we would get scared, and she was right. I was terrified for nearly a whole year after seeing a dead body for the first time. I knew she wouldn't want me and my brother to see her the way she was and that she wouldn't have wanted us to be around the chaos in Trinidad.

***

I've had a year to reflect on everything that has happened, and while I may not show it, it's something that stays with you. This past February and March were also difficult ones with the protests against gender violence. My grandmother's photo was plastered onto a poster among a number of other women's photos and strung by the Red House. Strangers, people I did not know, made signs with her name on them saying, "Remember Daiyke Mongroo." It was a mix of emotions; kind and touching that although none of my family could be there to protest, these strangers were bravely doing so. But it was also triggering because we are victims, which made it more real.

I'm not ignorant of the plight that Indo-Caribbean women face. I've grown up around the spews of domestic violence and gender stereotypes, but in going through this incident, I became privy to both of these issues as they relate to Trinidadian women. While similar, the plight endured by immigrant families, such as my own, is different from those that didn't leave. Women don't have access to resources like therapy, domestic violence shelters, and in some cases, basic education. If they are lucky enough to have access to these resources, it's still considered taboo to use them. The country is racially divided, causing even more rifts among people.

My grandmother's plight was no different. At 16, she had an arranged marriage to my grandpa. Shortly after, both she and my grandpa endured a series of traumatic experiences, for which they both blamed themselves. Not knowing how to deal with their trauma, they both tried the best they could and eventually started a family, having my dad and my aunt. My grandma was very protective of her children. She had a great skill for reading people's intentions. She knew when someone was "*Fooling You.*" "*Friends will carry you, but they'll never bring you back,*" was her favourite proverb. You just couldn't lie to her, she saw right through you, sometimes to a fault, but no one is perfect. She was someone who lived to take care of others, but oftentimes I wonder how she took care of herself. She was so strong. She never let anyone see her battles or fight them for her. She always kept her head held high and wasn't afraid to put anyone in their place.

Don't get me wrong, Trinidad is a beautiful country. I mean, look at all those strangers who came out to protest for my grandmother and the other women. That alone shows the spirit of these people. They deserve better. Women in Trinidad, Guyana, and all other Indo-Caribbean countries deserve better. They deserve a government that takes prosecuting crimes against women seriously and leaders that don't take away basic rights when they see a chance to profit. They deserve to know that they matter, a state that doesn't give privileges to just the rich.

The saddest part is the majority of these victims' families, including myself, probably won't get justice due to the lack of stability in Trinidad. It takes years to prosecute certain crimes, and as a result, witnesses pass away or retract their statements during that time, making prosecutor's jobs more difficult. Most of these cases become cold if the media doesn't give your case attention.

I'm in a better place than most of these families. I'm in a place where I am going to be a lawyer, the first female lawyer in my family. I have opportunities that these families do not that these victims could not dream of. My grandmother's wish to see her children succeed came true. She got to meet her grandchildren; she got to raise them, see them grow up and experience the world. Some of these women didn't live to see their 21st birthday. My dad has a family. He's worked hard to give us the things we want. My aunt is the same. We're not rich, but we're not head above water either. We are happy. And while murder doesn't discriminate based on socioeconomic status, our situation could be a lot worse.

This is why it's important for us as first-generation Indo-Caribbean women to work hard and give back. If you can make a change, why not do that? Why not help your people? I mean, these are the same people that got you here. Too often in our Indo-Caribbean community, we discriminate against our own—and for what? Because someone is doing better than you? It's time to end that because there's a bigger problem going on here.

My message to young Indo-Caribbean women is to work hard. Don't give up on your dreams. Don't listen to the people that tell you that you can't do it because you can. Your ancestors are watching you and they want you to succeed. I never thought I'd end up becoming a lawyer, but I was put in this position for a reason and I'm going to use it to benefit others. Your immigrant families have worked too hard to see you lose, and if you think it's too late to start again, it isn't. I promise you it isn't. *"Once you have your education, no one can take that away from you,"* is something my Grandma would always say. Make your families proud.

I hope that one day after I've settled in my legal career and my blogging career, I can open a non-profit that helps fund women's education in Trinidad.

***

It's still hard for me to wrap my head around what's happened, but I know slowly, things will begin to make sense. After Winter break, I came back to my apartment and could not stop thinking about what we had gone through. I had trouble sleeping (I still sometimes do), and every day I couldn't stop thinking, *did this really happen?* My friends really supported me throughout the way. My law school friends sent me notes, their outlines, and whatever I needed just to help me end my semester. They checked in with me and called me. My friends from home sent me flowers and called me asking if they could bring me and my brother food. I've never felt more loved.

I'm no longer afraid of the smaller things like being called on in class. If there's anything this experience has taught me, it's that I am strong. I am strong enough to get through whatever is thrown my way. Yes, I still feel those common feelings of stomach knots and my throat tightening when something scary arises, but I know that I'll be okay. This mindset helps me overcome anything I am scared about. I've matured.

Perhaps the biggest lesson I've learned is that life doesn't stop for anyone when things get hard. You have to move with it; otherwise, you won't catch up. You get busy with life for a while, and then you remember: *I'm in my final year of law school, graduating in May of 2022.* I know amidst the pain my dad feels, he cannot wait to see me get my Juris Doctor in May. I know he'll feel like all his troubles have ended because he can brag to everyone that his daughter is a lawyer.

I know that once the high of it all winds off, he'll remember the way he lost his mom. He'll remember that she couldn't be here to see this, and he may be sad for some time, but he'll be okay. Life continues and he has to continue with it.

More or Less Indian

Alisha Persaud

From: Office Manager

To: 5th Floor Staff

Subject: *Diwali* Celebration

Dear all,

      Please join us at 3 p.m. Wednesday afternoon in the conference room for light refreshments courtesy of some of our colleagues celebrating Diwali, the Festival of Lights!

If you'd like to contribute, please contact Sam.

Wow, I love this job! I've only been here a few months, but we've already had a day off for Eid and now we're observing Diwali in the office. This is exactly what I hoped for when I started working at the United Nations—inclusion and mutual respect.

Reaching into my bag, I lean to ask my deskmate, "Prithi, how much are most people giving toward the Diwali thing?"

Prithi keeps clicking on her keyboard. "I'unno. I gave twenty."

"Awesome. Thanks."

I fish out a twenty-dollar bill and start strutting towards Sam's cubicle around the corner. I chuckle at my gait; I've seen it on this floor since I first started. The swagger of belonging, what was traditionally an American white male privilege, is now displayed with equal confidence on a floor populated with Filipinos, Ukrainians, Mayalsians, Haitians, Chinese, and Ethiopians, to name a few, and of course, South Asians. And now one grinning Indo-Caribbean-American.

"Hey, Sam." Sam is one of the only Desis on the floor to still use the Anglicized version of his name, Samrat. Probably a remnant of his prior years in corporate America.

"Hi, Sharon."

My parents gave me an English name to spare me the discrimination they experienced when they came to New York. Even my very Guyanese last name, Persaud, was often mistaken by my school teachers to be of French origin. That was early in the Indo-Caribbean exodus to New York before we took over Queens.

Holding the twenty-dollar bill forward, I say, "I wanted to contribute towards the Diwali thing." Sam stares blankly into my face. "On Wednesday?" Blink. "Or is it too late?"

Sam says, "You don't have to, " Narrowing his eyes meaningfully."

"Thanks, but I want to."

Still looking confused, Sam proffers another out. "No, I mean, it's only for the Indian people."

I feel a twinge of ... something. I freeze my smile. I'll give him the benefit of the doubt—maybe my English first name and French-sounding last name confused him.

"Right," I say, stretching my hand more toward him for emphasis. "So, *here*."

Then he says it. Aloud. To my face. "But you're not Indian."

It's my turn to blink. Only one word escapes me. "What?"

"You're not Indian."

"Ahm." How do *I* do this diplomatically? "Yes. I *am*."

"But you're not *from* India."

Blink, blink. Is this actually happening at the U.N.? "But all my *foreparents* are."

"Really? Where in India are they from?"

"Well, we don't actually know, but most of the migrants were from U.P." Maybe if I use the common abbreviation for Uttar Pradesh, he'll see that I'm Indian enough to know that much.

"So you've never been there." He leans back in his chair as though he's made his point.

"No." What is this? U.S. Border Patrol? Am I applying for a visa? Citizenship?

"And you don't speak the language." THE language? Desis speak Hindi, Tamil, Telugu, Malayalam, and Gujarati on our floor alone.

"I speak English, but I'm still Indian." I feel heads turning, but I continue.

He smiles as if explaining to a child. "But you're not."

I shove my arm forward and tap the crook of my elbow. "Do you want to check my blood?" I'm getting louder, but I don't care at this point. "All of my great-grandparents were born in India. That makes me Indian." Needing this to end, I firmly extend the twenty-dollar bill and ask, "Do you want it or not?"

"No, that's ok."

"Fine." I spin on my heel and storm back to my cubicle.

I'm too … something (Angry? Hurt? Disappointed? All of the above?) to realize the interrogation wasn't about whether I am Hindu or whether I observe Diwali. Needing something else to focus on, I unlock my computer only to see a new email from Sam.

Dear Sharon,

Sorry, I offended you. If you'd still like to contribute something, we would happily accept it.

I scoff. One of the other (nicer) Desis seated near him must have informed him that he was being an ass. I ponder for a minute before conceding to my heart. This isn't about Sam; it's about Diwali. So I walk back to his desk and hold out the money.

Looking a tiny bit contrite, Sam takes it. "Sorry again, Sharon."

Pressing my lips together, I nod and return to my desk. *United Nations*, huh?

***

Prithi arrives Wednesday morning with several shopping bags, which she stows under her desk.

"Morning."

"Hey Prithi, early morning shopping?"

"No, I just brought some stuff from home to decorate the conference room for this afternoon. Wanna help? Some of us are going to set up during lunch." She sits and logs in to her computer.

I smile inside. This is how it should be.

"Sure! I'd love to."

***

One Year Later

> From: Office Manager
>
> To: 5th Floor Staff
>
> Subject: Diwali, the Festival of Lights
>
> Dear All,
>
> > Join us Thursday afternoon in the conference room at 3:00 p.m. for refreshments in celebration of Diwali - courtesy of your colleagues! If you'd like to contribute, please contact Sam or Sharon.

"Hey, Sharon," Osondu calls over our cubicle divider.

In the past year, I've made more friends in the office. Mostly non-Desis because I found there are more Indian folks who think like Sam once did. However, Sam has been excessively friendly, still overcompensating for that initial blunder—like asking me to help with this year's Diwali event.

I kick off to roll my chair to where I can see Osondu. "What's up?"

"You gonna do a Diwali dance on Thursday?"

Over his shoulder, a few heads have turned, including Sam's. "Sssshhh!" Only a handful of folks at the office know about this.

But in exuberant Osondu fashion, he doesn't lower his voice. "You should totally do a dance. Vikram is gonna sing again, right? So you should dance."

Sam strolls over. "You dance, Sharon?"

I admit, "Yeah, a little, trying to downplay it."

Prithi jumps in. "A little? You've been doing it for what, twenty years?"

Sam is surprised, "Wow! Twenty years! I had no idea! What kind of dance?"

I name two of the classical dance forms of South India. "Bharatanatyam and Kuchipudi."

Sam's eyes light up. "We can organize a cultural presentation—singing and dancing. Everyone would love it. You'll do it?"

Prithi and Osondu both answer for me, "Yes!"

***

Thursday, I wear a white *kurti* and *dupatta*, thick *kohl* on my eyes, and even a sticker bindi. I've performed hundreds of times for all types of crowds, but today I'm unsettled. I feel like I'm about to be judged by those Desis who throw dismissive glances and speak their dialects to each other when I'm in the breakroom or elevator with them. Ugh, why do I even care so much?

Sam recites the story of the *Ramayana* as it relates to Diwali, the one about lamps being lit to herald Rama's triumphant return to *Ayodhya* after 14 years of exile. I can't help wondering if I would be welcomed "Home" as well, and I am annoyed with myself for even thinking about it. I find Prithi and Osondu in the crowd alongside my other international friends—my own little unity of nations—all grinning ear to ear. Osondu is literally vibrating with excitement. It warms my heart.

As Sam announces me, I invoke my training to clear my head. I begin as always, showing the gestural cues while explaining the narrative, which echoes the end of the tale just told: Rama defeats his enemy and rescues his wife, Sita, before journeying home to Ayodhya to reign as king.

The demonstration is complete; I realize the room is silent. Even the disdainful Desis are paying casual attention, but I forget even them as the Carnatic flute swells and fills my being. Melody, *mridangam* and movement merge as I launch into the storytelling.

Rama, his wife Sita, and his brother Lakshmana are all living in exile in the forest.

Rama goes hunting and Sita, hearing a cry for help, sends Lakshmana to assist.

Before leaving, Lakshmana creates a protective circle around Sita.

Once alone, Rama's enemy arrives in disguise, tricking Sita into leaving the circle of protection and kidnapping her.

I see nods of recognition for parts in the demonstration in my peripherals and know I've managed to connect to even those not familiar with the tale beforehand.

Rama's supporters help build a bridge to cross to the island nation where Sita is being held captive.

Rama battles his enemy and finally wins, freeing Sita. But before leaving the island, Sita endures a literal trial by fire to prove that she remained pure throughout her captivity.

She emerges unscathed, and together they travel toward their homeland. The people of Ayodhya rejoice at their return, and Rama finally assumes the throne with Sita by his side.

As the flute fades and I bring my awareness back to the room, I feel warmth beaming at me. Desi and non-Desi alike are leaning in, saying things like "I had no idea you could do that," "That was really cool," and Osondu's "Maybe you can teach me some moves." People who did not deign to acknowledge my presence in the room before were now looking me in the eye and smiling.

As everyone mingles over samosas and chai, I can't help feeling vindicated like I won a victory today for Indo-Caribbeans. I survived my trial by fire and proved that we remained true to our Indianness, and the people of our ancestral homeland welcomed us back.

And yet …

***

A Few Years Later

I'm still at U.N., as are Sam and Osondu. I still dance for every office Diwali celebration. There have, of course, been changes as well. I've made many new Desi friends—like Vedant, who accepts it at face value when I say I'm Guyanese *and* Indian, just as Prithi did.

But there is also a fresh crop of Desis here under a new contract. Vedant makes it a point to introduce me to them by saying, "Sharon's more Indian than me!" Once again like all those years ago, my eyes narrow to examine my features. My ears prick up to detect any regional accent. Eventually, my lips curl condescendingly like I'm a child playing make-believe.

The fact that Vedant even feels the need to introduce me the way he does means he *knows*. He's trying to shield me from the stigma assigned to the diaspora —the persistent belief that we've lost our Indianness by violating some antiquated proscription against crossing the "Kala Pani." Ironically, the very people assigning the stigma to Indo-Caribbeans have themselves crossed the Kala Pani and did so of their own volition.

Remember Sita in the story I had danced for that Diwali years ago? Like her, we were tricked, kidnapped and carried away to a distant land with no means to return on our own. We, too, preserved the ties we carried in our hearts—she for her husband, us for our motherland. Like Sita, we longed for home.

But we had no Rama coming to rescue us. So we adapted in order to survive. We preserved what we could, but we also assimilated. That means we speak only English and have Anglicized names for many of us. Does this make us less Indian?

I know when Vedant vouches that I'm *more* Indian than him, he means well. But why is there even a scale of Indianness?

I then realized I was using the very same scale. When I was challenged by Sam years ago, I argued that the fact that all my foreparents were born in India as proof of my Indianness. If I were of mixed ancestry, would that have justified his claim? And those other Desis that only recognized my heritage after I danced— would they be right to exclude me if I hadn't studied an Indian art form intensively? Of course not.

So what is the threshold? I think back to Sita's story, which did not end with Rama's coronation as it did in the dance. Sita's virtue during her captivity is challenged yet again in some versions, and she is banished from Ayodhya—even though she passed the trial by fire when she was first rescued. In every version of the story, Sita's actual faithfulness is irrefutable. The accusation of one low-minded individual leads to her banishment—based on the *perception* of infidelity. A quality attributed to her from others —undeservedly and despite all proof to the contrary.

So I ask myself: If no evidence could be enough to thwart Sita's unjust expulsion, what proof would be enough for us?

This is when I realize that the adequacy of proof is not the issue. The problem is that there is any test at all. Why imbue others with authority to validate who I am, who we are? We knew who we were since we first crossed the oceans in 1838. We knew it still when we crossed again over 100 years later to settle in New York, London, Toronto and beyond. Today, almost 200 years and two continents later, I remain as innately Indian as I am also Caribbean and American. These are not mutually exclusive. Being more than "just Indian" does not make us less Indian. We never have to prove that to anyone.

The Struggle is Real
Nadia Persaud

The seam of the roti was hot as I flipped it with my bare hand. Crispy flakes
flew across the makeshift kitchen as the roti landed on the *tawa*. Sweat
collected on my forehead; I never could stand the heat. A pot of oil bubbled
beside me and I pushed the golden plantain around with a pot spoon, ladling
the oil to make them fry evenly.

"Jaya, hurry up; Nah, man!"

Mom's voice carried over the steady steel drum beat that floated
between the flea market stalls and the loud chatter that filled the air. Bright,
glittery lehengas hung from the ceiling and gold costume jewellery twinkled
under the yellow industrial lights.

I snuck a peek over my shoulder. A long line was forming in front of
our food stall—hungry people. People who looked like they would fight if
they weren't fed in time. Taking a deep breath, I pulled the roti from the tawa
and clapped, the heat burning the tips of my fingers. I clenched my teeth,
wanting to drop it, but that would mean I'd have to start again.

When the roti was soft and flaky, I folded it neatly, placed it into the styrofoam container with goat curry and potatoes, and brought it to the counter.

"Goat curry and roti!" I yelled. A man wearing sunglasses and a heavy coat approached, took the container and nodded his thanks.

"Stay up here. Me gah cook," Mom said to me, tightening her apron around her waist.

She was a much better cook than I'd ever been.

As I moved receipts and loose papers aside to find a pen to take orders, an envelope with bright red print caught my eye.

To: Shanta Ramdin, Shanta's Kitchen

From: Dr. Flea's Flea Market

EVICTION NOTICE

I swallowed the growing lump in my throat. I'd deal with it later, now wasn't the time. I turned to the next customer and smiled sweetly.

"What can I get you?"

***

"When were you going to tell me?" I asked, slamming the door to our tiny apartment shut so hard that the doorframe rattled.

"Tell yuh wat, Jaya?"

Mom had her back to me, her voice tired and drained.

I slid the chain across the door and pulled the envelope from my jeans pocket. "That we're being evicted from our stall!"

Stepping in front of her, I waved the paper in her face. She furrowed her brows and snatched it from my hands. "Nah, worry about it. I have it under control."

I followed her into the kitchen. "How is it under control if we're being evicted? How much do we owe?"

"I said Nah, worry," Mom said a little more sternly. She huffed and turned the kettle on to make herself a cup of tea.

"If you need money, you can tell me. I'll help you."

She ignored me, opening and shutting the cupboards with a heavy hand. Any harder and the doors might fall off.

"Mom, do you need money?"

"I nah need money. I need yuh fah to play de lottery."

I leaned against the fake marble counter and rolled my eyes.

When I was sixteen, Mom visited her sister in Guyana and had my birth chart read by a pandit. The very first thing she told me when she returned was that I was going to be a millionaire. I found it hard to believe. The chances of me winning the lottery were one in a million. More likely not to happen than to happen. I'd never even bought a lottery ticket.

"How much do we owe?"

Mom didn't look at me as she poured hot water into her mug, her shoulders hunched. "Five hundred dollars."

My breath caught in my throat. Five hundred dollars? That was at least a month's rent at the flea market. I didn't even have that much in my bank account.

Maybe it was time to start looking for a serious job. I graduated from university a year ago, but I hadn't had any luck with getting a job. And then things...changed and I had to help Mom at the flea market stall. Family first.

I licked my lips. "How long are they giving us to pay them?"

"Two weeks," Mom said flatly.

Two weeks. *Two weeks*. We could work with that. We had no choice.

Carefully, I approached Mom and wrapped my arms around her chest. Her back pressed against me, her brown skin warm against mine. Her black hair smelled like coconut oil. I pressed a kiss to the top of her head.

"We'll find the money somehow."

***

I stuffed my earbuds into my ears, blasted my music, and kept my head down as I pushed the rickety janitor cart. I made myself as small and as invisible as I could. There weren't many workers in the office at 7 p.m., but I didn't want to disturb the few that were.

Picking up a trash can by a desk, I dumped its contents; scraps of paper, a banana peel, and broken rubber bands into the larger can on my cart and replaced the bag to the beat. I gave the surface of the desk a quick dusting with the duster and moved to the next.

Time slipped by quickly as I worked. I didn't have to think too much. It was like being on autopilot. Dump, spray, swipe, repeat. I'd be finished in another two hours. I'd just have to clean all seven floors and put the dishes in the dishwasher in the kitchen. Then I could go home and sleep.

I rolled the cart along with the carpeted floors. I took this job because I was desperate. Our bills were stacking up and I still hadn't found a job. Now I spent the day with Mom at our *Shanta's Kitchen* stall at the flea market and cleaned the offices of an automotive company at night.

I worked silently, the music pounding in my ears keeping me going. As I wiped down a desk, a brown woman in pinstripe pants and a white blouse stood up in her cubicle; a handbag draped across her arm. Her black hair was tied in a tight bun. I couldn't see her face. Her back was to me.

I looked back down at the desk, wiping it down with lemon-scented spray.

"Jaya?"

I spun around, pulling my earbuds away from my ears.

"Shanaya?"

My arms and legs congealed like *dhal* that had been left on the stove for too long.

"Oh, wow. It's so nice to see you. What are you doing here?"

I swallowed.

Shanaya Sharma and I met at the university. We had a couple of classes together.

I was suddenly aware of the navy vest I was wearing, branded with the pink *Molly Maid* logo.

"Nice to see you too! I, uh, I...I'm working."

Shanaya's eyebrows flew up in surprise. "Oh." She paused. She was thinking. "I know how this sounds, but I never thought you'd end up here. You were, like, the smartest person in our class."

I recoiled slightly, blinking. She didn't lay a hand on me, but it was like she'd slapped me.

"Yeah, well...things change. My dad...my dad left. My mom and I were left with the bills. I applied to so many positions, but I wasn't getting hired. I needed a job that would cover some of the payments we had to make, so that's why...I'm here."

Why was I telling her all this? We hadn't spoken in years. She didn't need my sob story. She probably had more important things to do than stand around talking to me about how my drunkard father walked out on us. No warning. Dad and Mom would fight endlessly about his drinking. He never wanted to change. He didn't even text us or call. He didn't leave a note. He packed a suitcase and we found out days later he was staying with his brother.

"Are you having money problems?" Shanaya whispered.

I shrugged my shoulders. "Sort of."

She adjusted the strap of her handbag. She was thinking again. "If you want, I could try to get you a job here. We need data analysts."

I looked up from the carpeted floors. "Seriously?"

Shanaya nodded. "Yeah. You've got the experience. Give me your number. I'll put in a good word for you."

Numb, I handed her my phone and we exchanged numbers.

"I'll be in touch soon."

"Thanks," I mumbled, not entirely believing what happened.

***

By the time I got home, a bright smile on my face, Mom was seated at the small kitchen table with her evening cup of tea, a slice of plain bread, and an opened tin of sweetened condensed milk. A butter knife balanced precariously on the tin, drops of milk dripping down the sides.

I took off my sneakers and pecked her on the cheek. "Good news!"

"Oh?" Mom said absentmindedly as I went straight to the fridge for something to eat. I picked up margarine containers filled with curry, pumpkin, and *bhaji*. I squinted against the light, deciding between the three dishes.

"One of my old classmates works at that office I clean and I didn't even know. I guess she was staying late for something. She said she's going to try and get me a job."

"Dat nice."

Nice? We wouldn't have to worry about making rent at the flea market if I got this job. If we were ever behind, I could pay the difference. We wouldn't ever have to worry about money again with the increased income.

Shutting the fridge, I stood in front of her.

The eviction letter had been opened and the unfolded paper was in her hands. "Mom, what's wrong?"

She lifted her face. Fine wrinkles lined her eyes. She looked exhausted. "I thought dis letter was because me Nah pay de rent, but Jaya, dey selling de whole damn flea market. We all have to leave in two weeks' time."

"What? Why?"

"Sum shipping company buy de place out. Dey building warehouses."

I fell into the chair opposite her, too stunned to speak.

Our entire livelihood had just been pulled from beneath our feet.

"Oh lord," Mom wailed, her head in her hands. "Wah we gah do, Jaya? How we gah pay de bills?"

I shook my head. "I don't know, Mom."

I couldn't mess up this job interview. It was our only hope now.

***

"To tell you the truth, Jaya, there's only one thing holding me back from hiring you."

I was seated across from a brown man with salt and pepper hair. He was dressed in a perfectly unwrinkled button up and his loafers peeking out from beneath the desk looked like they were freshly polished. I was so nervous; I'd already forgotten his name.

The interview went as well as it could. I'd answered all his questions thoughtfully and with poise. I showed that I could get results.

"Oh?" I said, trying to keep the fear from my voice.

I *needed* this job. Mom and I were an inch away from bankruptcy with the flea market shutting down and our stall with it. Cleaning offices wasn't going to cut it.

"There's a huge gap after your graduation. You haven't actually held a job with any kind of experience this role requires. It's a risk for me to take you on."

I swallowed. What do I say to that? Was it even worth bringing up my family life? That Dad left?

"I understand. I had some...difficult circumstances to navigate with my family at that time. But it's all calmed down now. And I can assure you; that I'm a fast learner. I can pick up on whatever I need to do quickly. I have the knowledge, and I'll have the skills with a little practice."

I released a shaky breath. That was the best I could do apart from falling down on my knees and begging for the job.

The man smiled at me, the corners of his eyes crinkling. "Those are all the questions I have for you. Do you have any for me?"

I asked a couple of generic questions about the workplace culture just to show I was interested and then we were standing, shaking hands.

"It was a pleasure to meet you, Jaya. I'll be in touch soon."

"It was a pleasure to meet you, too..." Mr. I forgot your name.

"Thank you for your time."

I left his office feeling like he held my future in his hands.

***

The vacuum roared as I cleaned the carpets of the office I had interviewed in just a week before. I still hadn't heard back from the man about whether or not I got the job. I assumed that meant I didn't and that meant Mom and I were in trouble. She was still working at the stall, trying to get as many sales as possible before the flea market was shut down for good.

I was on the top floor of the office. My headphones hung around my neck, dangling like two long stalks of *bora*. It was almost 9 p.m. There wasn't a sign of anyone left in the office, the computer screens dark and drawers locked up.

I finished and did my final sweep of the floor in fifteen minutes, making sure I didn't miss anything. I dragged the cart and vacuum back to the janitorial closet, locked up, and took the elevator back down to the main lobby.

By the time I'd found my beaten-up car in the parking lot, my entire body was achy and sore. I had to lug myself to the door.

I would be cleaning offices for the rest of my life.

Turning the key, the engine came to life. I got about halfway home before I realized that the tank was almost out of gas. My eyelids were heavy, threatening to close. I flicked the indicator on and pulled into a gas station.

I dug around in my wallet and found forty dollars. That would have to be enough. I leaned against the car, sleepy, as I filled the tank.

From above the hood, I peeked into the gas station store. The green and blue Lotto Max sign read: $50,000,000 in red lights. It will be drawn this Saturday.

I glanced at the meter. I released the pump and screwed the tank cap back on when it got to thirty-five dollars.

Marching into the store, I hurried up to the cashier. "Pump three, please."

The woman read the total I owed and I handed her the cash. "Give me a Lotto Max ticket too, please."

I barely recognized my voice as I handed over the remaining five dollars. The woman printed the ticket and slid it across the counter towards me.

I just stood there, staring at the seven numbers for a moment.

27 7 8 2 40 42 18

"Here's your receipt."

I jumped, forgetting where I was and rushed out of the store, tucking the ticket into my wallet.

I don't know what I was expecting, but it cost me five dollars that could have gone towards a bill.

***

Early on Saturday morning, before the sun had risen, Mom and I headed to the flea market to clean out our stall. I stood on a stool and unpinned the *Shanta's Kitchen* banner, rolling it up and setting it aside. Mom would probably throw it away. What purpose could it serve now?

We'd already sold all the appliances to a couple of buyers. At least that money would hold us over until we figured out what we were going to do next.

I loaded a blender into a cardboard box. Bags of flour and potatoes and chickpeas had already been packed up onto a trolley that we'd wheel out to the car later.

Our stall was bare and barren, stripped of its counters and display cases. Wiping my brow, I looked up to find Mom with her arms crossed, deep in conversation with our stall neighbours, a couple who sold bubble tea. They all shook their heads, gesturing around the food court.

If Mom was taking a break, I would too. I leaned against the brick wall and scrolled through my social media accounts. I liked a couple of posts and then froze. Someone in Brampton won the $50,000,000 jackpot.

I stuck my hand into the pocket of my jeans. Where was my ticket? Where did I put it?

I frantically searched for it before remembering I'd put it in my wallet. I dug the thin, crumpled paper out and went to the lottery website, barely catching a full breath. When I found the winning numbers page, I read each number, carefully comparing it to my ticket.

27...27.

7...7.

8...8.

2...2.

40...40.

42...42.

Oh my god! I was six for six!

18...18.

Did I just win the lottery? I scanned the numbers again. Then again. And again. Every single number matched.

A sob escaped my throat and I hurriedly clapped a hand over my mouth as tears dropped onto my cheeks.

My fingers shook as I picked up a pen and signed my name on the paper, claiming the ticket. Claiming my wealth.

"Mom!" I shouted.

She whipped her head around at me, clearly annoyed. "What?"

"Come here!"

"Jaya—"

"Come here!"

Smiling at our former stall neighbours, she took her to leave and stood in front of me. "What yuh want?"

I couldn't keep the grin from spreading across my face. "I won the lottery," I whispered.

"What?" Mom screeched, her eyes bulging from her head.

"I won $50,000,000." I handed her the ticket.

She clutched it to her chest and sobbed.

"Oh, Jaya," she whimpered.

"I know, Mom." I gathered her hands in mine.

We'd never have to struggle again.

Shades of Caramel

Savita Prasad

It is the responsibility of non-Black folks to learn the history and experiences of Black people outside of the region they reside in and assess race relations on an individual and community level. Anti-Blackness is evident in all cultures. The media manipulates how African lands are perceived, refusing to acknowledge the richness and beauty of the continent. The concept of Blackness is nuanced outside the United States. We are bound to interact with Black individuals in the diaspora and of different ethnicities and have to put in the work to see not only the individuals, but how their experiences were shaped by systemic oppression and colonization. Because of colonialism, there is no single look for a group or nationality of a person. The African diaspora is scattered across the world, including countries in Latin America and Caribbean islands that the Spanish colonized, British, Dutch, and French.

The pain behind our ancestors' history is far from forgotten. Acknowledging the heavy burdens they carried is the first step to healing intergenerational traumas and standing in solidarity with communities outside of our own ethnicities. As non-Black Caribbeans, we could easily bond over a shared culture while still unknowingly perpetuating anti-Blackness or ignoring the existence of racial tensions by simply pretending it does not exist. Caribbean culture was built on systems our ancestors were forced into. Much of Indo-Caribbean culture is drawn from Afro-Caribbean culture. In fact, it was the Africans who taught the Indians English when they first arrived in the Caribbean. The melting pot of West Indian culture created common grounds between races removed from their ancestral roots. Soca and other musical genres, *Creolese*, shared foods, cultural practices and traditions, and much more are a byproduct of the cultural mashup.

It is essential to stand in unity and uphold ourselves with accountability to dismantle white supremacy. Raised in survival mode, we've kept our heads down and focused on our work as per the advice of our elders, assimilating to a society that values capitalism. It is the denial of our palatability and the role in adhering to expectations of the model minority myth that keeps anti-Black institutions in place. Without taking into consideration ethnic backgrounds, people automatically group Indo-Caribbeans with South Asians and Afro-Caribbeans with other Black people when these individuals emigrate to North America. As we know, Black people, regardless of ethnicity, face a violent reality around the world. Taking off the lenses we wore in our childhood and trying on an upgraded prescription of which we actively unlearn stereotypes allows us to have a clearer vision of the world. To break the cycle, we must learn from the past and have plans set in motion to address the issues that continue to plague us today.

***

The brisk air circulating from the fan's whirling blades was a welcome relief to their sticky caramel skin. Jay looked over at a giddy Devi, who mirrored his Cheshire smile.

"How are we going to top off last year's anniversary?"

"We could spend it right here and keep doing this." Devi rolled on top of him, straddling his body and started a trail of slow kisses down his neck. She smiled as she heard a light chuckle arise from his chest.

"We could do that... and then have your Ajee over for dinner afterward? I'll cook."

Caught off guard, the shock of the suggestion repelled her back. She scrambled to mask her frantic thoughts and string together the right words to mollify the apprehension settling in between them. Whenever he mentioned Ajee, she withdrew. Jay stared into her chocolate brown eyes and gently laced their fingers together. She was in his arms, but her mind was elsewhere.

Devi's eyes fixated on their hands. "Ajee doesn't want to leave the comfort of her house and she hates it when we push her in the wheelchair. I don't even think our apartment complex is accessible. She won't be able to enter the building without the assistance of a ramp."

"So then let's have dinner at her house."

The lump in her throat thickened. "Okay."

Her stomach was in knots. The constricting feeling in her chest intensified. As Jay caressed her arms, Devi saw two different shades of caramel.

"I have to talk to her first." She feigned a smile, but her rapid heartbeats were throbbing in her ears.

The walls of their bedroom were enclosing her. Devi was spinning around, seeing everything and nothing all at once. Leaving Jay in their bed, she went to the bathroom and turned on the faucet of the shower. Inhaling deeply through her nostrils and exhaling slowly through her lips, she tried to soothe herself. She stood still under the ice-cold water to immerse herself in the sensation.

The droplets of water rolling down her tanned hands took her back to summer vacations with her grandmother. Insecurity haunted her adolescence. She wanted to join other girls her age who ran across the beach in their two-piece swimsuits, leaving footprints in the damp dunes. She, too, wanted her skin to be kissed by the rays of sunshine. Instead, she was covered from head to toe. She wore a floppy creamy-hued hat falling over her eyes, an ivory-sleeved shirt that hid her hairy forearms, and cotton linen pants. The layers of sunscreen Ajee applied on her left her looking like the sister of Casper the ghost.

Under Ajee's instructions, a young Devi sat under an oversized beach umbrella on a mahogany-colored blanket. Ajee was the main attraction on the beach. People looked at her in a not-so discreet manner. She used to sit near the shorelines on her knees with her eyes closed and clasped hands over her head as she prayed. She ended the sacred rituals by pouring the water she collected from the waves over herself from a brass *lota*.

When they arrived home, Devi's regimen consisted of taking a shower to wash off her suntan. Ajee rubbed the irritating Fair & Lovely cream ferociously into her skin and joked about needing to bathe her in cow milk. While there were no ill intentions behind her pet name "Blackie," Devi felt displeased with her appearance. If her grandmother was concerned about her turning a few shades darker, would she be able to accept the man in her bed?

Devi's cousins in Guyana said it was different today. There were more interracial couples now, but Ajee left at the peak of racial tensions with no solution in sight. She carried more bitter than sweet memories. Ajee was from a different generation. She was born in the 1930s and married a man 20 years her senior—a man born during the indentured system designed by the British. With the British's attempt to eradicate their native tongue and the converting people to Christianity, colonialism left its mark on the diaspora.

Using the strategy to divide and conquer, the British imperialists planted the seeds of mistrust and created a power structure between marginalized groups to prevent a union that would overthrow them. Feeding lies to the disenfranchised groups, the stereotypes that Afro-Caribbeans were strong, but lazy, and Indo-Caribbeans were harvested, hardworking, but sly. After slavery was abolished, African descendants had four years of apprenticeship to provide plantation owners free labor until the Indians were brought in. Because Afro-Caribbeans were born into chattel slavery, they had no legal documents, education, or voting rights. It was difficult for them to obtain land. Resentment bloomed when the Indians came to take their place in the labor force. The indentured servants were granted minuscule wages and rationed food. The Indians were also "Free" in the sense that they kept a strained grip on the religions and cultures they brought with them as well as having the perk of owning a parcel of land at the end of their contract if they chose to stay.

Although they shared dehumanizing conditions, both groups had different intricately layered experiences. From being brought in on crammed ships riddled with deathly diseases, to brutalizing working conditions, to the lack of privacy from being pushed into the tiny slave barracks with others, to being treated as their master's property, assaulted, abused, and so much more. The Afro-Caribbean workers taught Creolese English to the Indo-Caribbeans they worked alongside on the sugar plantations. However, the British maintained a hierarchy to ensure a power struggle between the groups. The British assigned which jobs each race could have. Afro-Caribbeans were assigned positions, such as becoming field supervisors or authority figures who would have to curb indentured labour strikes with violence. Pitting minority groups against each other created ripples flowing to this day.

Nevertheless, former enslaved Africans and the recruited East Indian indentured servants joined forces in what was known as the Ruimveldt Riots to demand equal rights in government and society in 1905. Everything about Guyana was mixed up, but its politics. Left to rule themselves and on the verge of uniting their country with democratic socialist policies, Cheddi Jagan and Forbes Burnham created the Progressive People's Party (PPP) in 1950. After Guyana's independence in 1966, Britain abandoned the people it brought to the country. Foreign countries exploited the novice government party to serve their self-interests. United States President John F. Kennedy and his successors decided to prevent peace between the Indian and African descendants living in Guyana. The CIA was employed to meddle in Guyana's first election to prevent socialism during the Cold War. The United States and the United Kingdom supported Burnham's leadership in exchange for being the U.S.'s puppet, betraying Jagan in the process, and rejecting socialism. Burnham was elected with foreign support and formed the People's National Congress (PNC), a party based on communism and Afro-supremacy. Going rogue against the U.S., Burnham established ties with other communistic countries. The press was heavily censored during this time. He stole money from the treasury and imprisoned and killed journalists as well as his political opponents. His allies were given governmental jobs. The country eventually burned to the ground with state-sanctioned violence, economic collapse, and skyrocketing crimes with corruption in office when Desmond Hoyte entered.

Devi grew up listening to stories of the ban on imported foreign goods during Burnham's time. The country did not have wheat flour for roti and bread, staples in Indian households. The ration lines were long, and the shelves of the grocery stores were empty. Burnham's discrimination made life difficult for Ajee's generation. Indians were not offered equal opportunities and were shut out of higher education and civil service. Ajee's stories were traumatic.

She used to live in a town now called Linden until she had to leave. Being an Indian refugee haunted her. She could not escape the memories of her home engulfed by flames and the people beaten, brutalized, and murdered. Images of the petrified women caught, stripped down naked, and left on the streets after being raped were permanently sketched in her recollection. She was dragged by her hair. Her hair, a mark of beauty and a symbolic feature of being Indian was chopped without consent. She lost her husband in the chaos. She fled to safety with her children and never looked back. The ethnic cleansing of Indians in that town was known as the Wismar Massacre of 1964.

People today are rejoicing in each other's religious holidays, such as Eid, Diwali, Christmas, and the republic holiday, *Mashramani*. The melting pot of music, traditions, and food from different ethnic populations created West Indian culture. One people, one nation, one destiny. However, celebrations were interrupted whenever election season arrived, trailed by scandals. The political strife founded on race continues to this day. The two major parties focus on racial group preference over the well-being of their country.

Ajee decided she had enough during the 80s and decided to move to America with her children. She wanted to escape the perpetual cycle of poverty and its consequences. She was living in one of the Global South's poorest countries, despite an abundance of natural resources. The thought of everything Ajee went through and gave up pushed Devi to be her best. Ajee came to America with the clothes on her back and five dollars in her pocket. She also brought her fear of Black people along with her, a fact Devi did not pick up on until she was a teenager.

Having the privilege of growing up in a diverse neighbourhood in America, Devi grew up with Black friends. She was privy to conversations with friends who felt uneasy when going shopping or seeing a doctor. Devi wanted to support her friends. This did not take away Devi's love for her Indo-Caribbean culture, but she was aware of how some people were holding onto ideals that supported their proximity to whiteness over solidarity with Black people. She didn't share Jay's experiences, nor had she experienced the world as a Black woman and couldn't begin to understand the collective Black experience. All she could do was listen, stand in solidarity, confront her own fragility, and unlearn subconscious biases.

It was easy for Devi to call other people out. Colleagues who made problematic statements, such as "Why can't they protest peacefully?" or "Why are the protests violent?" got an earful about historical protests in a system that doesn't see you. She also confronted people who used the "N" word loosely. Yet, when it came to her own flesh and blood, Devi felt defeated and angry. The family was everything,, but she didn't want to choose between them and her person. How could she start a conversation with Ajee about anti-Blackness without dismissing her experience?

When Devi fell in love with Jay, she got a closer look at how the world treated him. All eyes were on Jay when she invited him to her *mandir* to celebrate *Phagwah*. The aunties' drawn-in eyebrows shot up at their first glance of him. He was used to staring in non-Black spaces, but Devi wasn't accustomed to the spotlight, the hushed whispers or the head tilts in their direction. She turned cherry red when she accidentally overheard the aunties telling her cousins not to talk to her or be seen with her. She didn't tell Jay about the incident. Since then, she hid him and avoided community and family events. Would Ajee react the same way, or would she be able to embrace him?

Devi struggled to fall asleep that night. The next morning, she woke up feeling queasy. Pots and pans were clanking together in the kitchen. The savoury whiffs of duck curry cooking in the hissing pressure pot on the stove would normally have her salivating. Instead, she was running to the toilet, dry heaving. Beads of sweat collected across her forehead as her newfound predicament dawned on her. Walking into the kitchen, she found herself smiling at Jay, who was holding a measuring cup.

"How much rum goes into the black cake?"

"You average it. Black cake is made with 4% fruit, and 96% is rum."

After a lengthy discussion with an excited and reassuring Jay, Devi gathered the courage to go see Ajee. She walked around to the back and let herself into the house to find Ajee weeping in the living room to the old Bollywood movie, *Dosti*. Ajee's little brown face was filled with crinkles that came with age, but her determined eyes showed she was a force to be reckoned with.

"Yuh put on."

"Hi to you too, Ajee." Devi trapped her in a bear hug.

"Suh wah new?"

"I want you to meet someone. We've been together for a while and it's serious. He's bringing food later."

"Leh meh see da starbai. Yuh knows meh get ah dream about fish." Ajee winked, but nerves were starting to take hold of Devi.

Her hands trembled as she handed her phone to Ajee to scroll through the pictures.

"This is Jay. I really like him."

Ajee unhooked her glasses from the gap between the buttons of her nightgown to take a closer look at Jay's photo. Her eyes widened. There it was that look.

They sat still, looking intently at each other. Ajee's quiet breaths overwhelmed Devi. She felt her throat closing up. Her heartbeats throbbed in her ears. The tears stinging her eyes were rolling down her face. Ajee sat there watching Devi quietly sobbing.

"I'm sorry," she whispered. Ajee turned away from her.

Devi's hands covered her abdomen. She hugged herself as Ajee slowly got up from the couch and caressed the walls for balance as she moved to her room.

Devi remained rooted in her seat as the hours flew by, staring at the white walls in a trance. When the doorbell rang, shockwaves passed through her, causing her to snap out of it. She could not get herself to move.

Ajee hobbled out of her room with an engraved jewellery box. She placed it on Devi's lap on her way to answering the door. Curious, Devi lifted the lid to find glittering gold Indian bridal jewellery.

"Hi, Ajee."

"Ah, duck curry meh smell?"

"I heard it was your favourite."

Mad

Anjali Seegobin

Blank walls stare back at me as I shuffle behind blue curtains. Mumbled sirens and dinging monitors play in the background. My body feels cold as I remotely step left, right, and left. I count my steps, my bones cracking and softening my breath with each move.

"So, what's your name?" No words left my mouth.

"I would like to help you, so your name would be a great start."

Chequered tiles of blue and green surround me; I inch forward like a pawn.

"Savitri."

He unfolds his legs and presses down on his clipboard as he writes my name. I peek at his name tag, Dr. David Hurtz. His black hair is slicked back with one strand cornering his left eye.

"Date of Birth?"

"April 10th, 1999."

"Okay, Savitri. I know this can be scary, but do you have any family I can call? Maybe a sister or an aunt?" My breath becomes shallow.

"Nobody I'd like you to call."

"According to your birthday, you're over 18. Are you sure there isn't someone I can call?" I didn't respond again.

"Would you like to tell me what happened?"

"Doctor, we'd like to check her vitals before you begin any questions," a nurse interrupts.

She's dressed in blue scrubs decorated with tiny dancing dolphins, matching her blue crocs. The nurse enters and begins checking my vitals, sliding a tight blood pressure strap along my noodle arms. She pumps the valve synchronously along with my heartbeat, tight enough to stretch the hairs on my skin.

"BP reads 120 over 80, pulse 75." Like Nish pretended to be a doctor, I smiled to myself and read my pulse. The nurse leaves and returns with a bright orange gown with wrinkles and strings. She pulls the curtains as I quickly change, my cold feet meeting the colder tile. I plop onto the hard bed, a wave of pain moving across my chest. *What am I doing here?* Tears begin to stream down my trembling cheeks. I don't know why I'm crying, but it feels like I need to. Doctor Hurtz passes by and offers a box of tissues.

"Are you ready to tell me what happened?"

I sniffle. He remains seated, tapping his clipboard with his pen. His white complexion is almost ghostly. I thought to myself, not me about to tell my problems to a white man.

"I just didn't feel good today."

"Can you explain further?"

"Um, I keep crying. I can't stop crying. How is it possible that I have so many tears?"

"Well, the human body is made up of about 60% water, so cry away."

I smiled. I forgot my facial muscles and remembered how to make such a gesture.

"There we go, a smile. So, where are you from?"

I reflected on my rehearsed explanation. Once upon a time, England decided to colonize a large portion of the world, specifically robbing my ancestors from their homes in India and bringing them to the Caribbean. They manipulated them into a system of indentured labour, leaving them oceans away from familiarity. My parents are from Guyana, descending from these labourers. I went for the easy answer.

"They're from Guyana."

"Where's Guyana?"

"In South America," I swear if he asks me if I speak—

"Do you speak Spanish?"

"Nope, Guyana is the only English-speaking country. But I am Indo-Caribbean."

"But Guyana is not in the Caribbean; it's in South America, right?"

Ah, I give up. "Simplified version, I was born in Queens, New York."

"Okay, so how did you end up here? What happened today?"

I hesitated, but wrestled with my need to speak. Suddenly Dr. Hurtz received a page and left in a rush, leaving me with a new doctor. I crossed my scuffed Stanley Smiths, eagerly waiting. A woman wearing a floral dress and a bright gold necklace opened my curtain. Her dark cranberry lipstick lined the cracks of her lips. She was brown, but was she my type of brown? My eyebrow peeked as I observed the way she carried herself.

"Hello dear, my name is Dr. Bisandilall."

Her West Indian card was confirmed, I thought to myself.

"I understand that Dr. Hurtz spoke to you prior; he had an emergency, so I'll be taking over now." I could hear the hidden Guyanese accent behind her forced American tone.

It felt comforting hearing a familiar voice, but daunting at the possibility of her knowing my family.

"I'm Savitri," I responded.

Should I trust her? Isn't patient-confidently a thing? If only Guyanese families knew what that was. Everyone's business is always their business to know; I wonder where that habit comes from.

"You can start by telling me why you decided to come here today," she spoke, tilting her metal glasses to glance at my eyes.

I felt intimidated, but assured that she was kind by the tone of her voice.

"Um, every time I wake up, it feels like the hardest thing to do. When I open my eyes, I dread the idea of moving. I'm reminded of everything I've lost, everything that isn't here anymore." More tears stream down as I struggle to breathe over my emotions. "I told my family; they told me I've run mad. That I just need to sleep or pray that I have nothing to feel upset about."

"Is your family Guyanese?" She asks with concern.

"Um, yes." At this moment, I was sure she was going to say she knew my mother's ajees picknen. I always hear people talk about back home in Guyana; everybody knows everyone and they lived so nicely together. Although this "Nice" blanketed many injustices.

"I was born in Guyana and raised back home where yuh can't hang yuh mouth unless you want licks. I grew up to understand the trauma my parents endured, which was passed on to me. They've been through so much, but it doesn't improve their response to trauma."

She gives me a half-smile as she begins writing on her clipboard. I immediately tensed up, shook by the thought of what she was writing.

"This morning, they came again like clockwork. Consuming me until I couldn't remember where I was. They strangled the voice out of me and I laid lifeless, defeated once again. I try not to disturb them or think about them. Once I do, it feels impossible to escape. It took me an hour to get back up and feel the ground again. I feel like it's my fault; I let the familiarity of hurt keep hurting me."

"How long has this been happening?"

"Over a year."

"Okay, I see. Can you walk me through your day before you got here?"

I froze suddenly, feeling a rush of fear. They're coming again; I can feel it. I quickly closed my eyes and began reflecting on my day

***

I glide my hot pink straightener down dark caramelized tones of fried hair robotically. Crackling noises arise as smoke fumes the air, forcing a small cough out of me. The sun begins peeking through my blinds at 6:30 a.m., my routine before school. I quickly plaited my hair as it roped down my back.

"Savitri, yuh like you eighteen going on twenty-five. School ah yuh fashion show? Dem picknen meh tell yah, force-ripe."

I ignored my mother's comments as I rushed out of the house. My hair was long enough that it swung by my knees. My parents, grandparents, uncles and aunts have troubled me about keeping it long. A woman's beauty is her hair, they'd repeat. Upon arriving at school, I was reminded of the beautiful teenagers around me with blonde hair, blue eyes and rich skin. My hair was frizzy, curly, oily and filled with knots. *How was that my beauty?* I thought.

"Hey Sav, we're going to have a sleepover at my house; want to come?" Samantha asks.

"Oh, uh, I can ask my parents." I didn't have to ask my parents; I knew the answer: "Yuh don't know these people, yuh can't trust people these days," I imagined mom would say. I quickly ran to my first-period class as I heard the bell echoed through the halls.

201- Environmental Science

I slid into my usual seat, acknowledging the one before me and the empty seat that a person no longer filled. All the memories of her daily breakfast sandwiches swarmed through me. She always left a trail of crumbs from the egg sandwich her mom made us. A tall man with circle glasses scurries inside and drops his leather bag on the desk. I wondered where my teacher might be; I had no idea who the stranger was.

"Okay, class, I'm going to be your substitute for today. We'll start with the attendance." He begins his roll call as I anticipate the mispronunciation of my name.

"Sah-sav-save-tee?"

"It's Savritri," I corrected him.

"Got it! Okay, Nisha? Is there a Nisha? Anyone?"

Suddenly, they're back again. I whisked away, tears streaming down as my body felt weightless. My stomach churned as I took a deep breath. The substitute's voice kept ringing in my ears.

"Nisha isn't here!" I scream.

Everyone spun around and 25 pairs of eyes glared at me as I sunk into my chair. I fought them off for the rest of the day until they progressively got louder. I wondered if anyone else understood how easy it was to be here, but not be present. That I walk around like a cell phone, searching for bars in a subway tunnel. After I floated through the rest of my classes, I wanted nothing more, but to sit at home, but it's never that easy.

"Savitri, you think yuh big woman now? How come yuh teacher dem tell me you holla pon dem? Who am I sending to this school? You nah do nothing in here fah guh school and misbehave! You must think I was born yesterday." As soon as I opened the door, I wanted to shut it.

"Mom, I've been having a hard time again. It feels hard to do things," I shrugged.

"You 18, what you know about hard, huh? Look, don't bother me right now."

"But, I've been having these thoughts again. I feel afraid sometimes," I stood frozen at the doorway, welcomed by photos of Lakshmi and Om signs.

The shoe rack stood below a picture of New Amsterdam Market and Kaieteur Falls in Guyana. Both illustrations served as a dualism for our complex identity.

"And what did I tell you? Do not tell your father this, do not tell anybody. Dem guh think yuh ran mad fah truth. You get great; the pandit told me last week when he opened the book. You were born on the wrong planet, so nah, tek worries, just go mandir on Sunday."

"I don't think it's helping me." My mother and aunt's favourite response to everything is picking up a book and reading or sitting down at the mandir.

"How you guh know if yuh nah try. You get one roof ova yah head, a plate of food every day, and yuh mother is alive. Just drink some Nutrophos and tea and catch yuh bed."

I stumbled into the kitchen, decorated with plastic fruits and fake flowers. The kitchen fridge was an ensemble of family photos from different family members. My eyes glazed over it, spotting a tall girl with ringlets. Nisha. They came back again, this time pulling at the remainder of the bread in my stomach. My food started to build up like a flood. I ran to the toilet, emptying out this morning's breakfast. I cradled my feet as I sat on the bathroom floor, crying again while my teeth chattered away. Every time they come, I somehow find comfort in knowing they always return. I saw a video telling me to welcome them to my table. To rid them, I had to befriend them. But this time, it only got worse; my stomach was sabotaging my appetite, burning my throat with each flood.

I can't do this anymore. I grabbed my keys and left the door unlocked.

***

Dr. B finished writing her sentence and glared up from her clipboard.

"So then you arrived here, at Presbyterian. Is this your first time in the psychiatric unit?" She asks.

"No."

I glanced at my lap, picking at my nails as she grilled me with questions.

"Have you been diagnosed or treated in the past?"

"Um, yes. But, I never got therapy or medication." My parents always warned me about drugs. If they knew I tried to take anti-depressants, I'd never hear the end of it.

"Why?"

"My parents never knew I was there. They thought I was on a school trip for three days.

I didn't know where else to go. I felt like a burden to everyone around me. I barely know who I am or what I am here for. How do I feel like myself? I don't even know anymore. These thoughts have been racking in my brain for as long as I can remember; only now they've gotten louder."

"When was the last time you felt like yourself?"

"I don't know. I guess with Nisha. My friend. She was my friend." I dug my nails into my palms as I felt them gnawing on my chest again.

"It's okay, Savitri, you're safe. We're at the hospital, just having a regular conversation. And what happened to Nisha?" Before I could answer, the curtain slid open.

"Savitri, what are you doing here?" Voice belts out.

My head swings around to find my 4'11" mother grappling with her purse. She looks flustered, breathing heavily as her sneakers squeak against the polished floors.

"A nurse called me. C'mon, we goin home."

"Ma'am, your daughter is here for treatment and she is over 18."

"Treatment for what? She's fine; there's nothing wrong with her."

"Mom, can you listen? Actually, listen for once. I'm staying." I never spoke back to my mother before; I grew anxious at the words that left my mouth.

"My name is Dr. Bisandilall. Your daughter has been experiencing some symptoms that have likely resulted from some trauma she's experienced." I felt a moment of relief like somebody cared and wanted to help me.

"I want my daughter out of here. Are you Guyanese? Don't you know better?" my mom yells.

"I realize that our culture would rather call us mad instead of seeing the woman fleeing abusive husbands or children left to raise themselves. We turn to our scriptures because it's what we've been taught, but healing is not a one-sided track. We come from a lineage of ancestors, uprooted from their homes and left to feign for themselves. They were forced into a laborious cycle, which has unfortunately left us to resist our emotions. They never had the option to receive help, but your daughter does."

My mom's body shifted, hands crossed, eyes staring at the floor.

"Alright."

I watched as her back turned, shoulders squared, walking through the exit. My heart sank, knowing she couldn't see the pain I've felt, knowing she felt like she was helping me in her own way. I'm sure I did something wrong in her head, but is it wrong to embrace how I feel? I've denied myself any agency to spare her the truth that I have depression and anxiety. I shouldn't be consistently sacrificing myself for the comfort of her beliefs.

"Savitri, we can take you inside the in-patient care now."

I follow Dr. B as we pass by an array of colourful doors. She smiles at me as I sense her hope. Her chamali perfume airs out the hallway as we stop in front of an oval doorway.

"We just have to finish some paperwork before we get you admitted, but this is your room. Our breakfast is every morning at 9 a.m., followed by medications. Then you'll meet with your psychiatrist."

"Um, I don't have any clothes besides the ones I came with."

"Do you think your mom can bring you some?" I didn't respond.

"It's okay; we can figure something out. I know it feels scary, but I promise that everything will fall into place."

I made my way into the green room, illustrated with flowers and honey bees. My mind felt quiet, almost uninterrupted by my thoughts. I sat down on the bed and noticed a small drawing by the bedframe. I began tracing my finger along the words carved inside,

N-I-S-H-A.

I smiled at the familiar name.

Liquid Gold

Samantha Raghunandan

"Latch na man," Tara said in an affectionate sing-songy voice tinged with fatigue.

Her left arm had begun to tingle with *jhun-jhun-nee* and she shifted her baby girl's position, carefully cupping the child's head and bottom as she did so. Switching a six-pound newborn from a "Football Hold" to "Cradle Old" with a half-asleep hand took some serious coordination, but Tara was learning quickly. She was mindful not to disturb the IV line taped to the top of her hand; it had been disconnected since last night, but had hurt *like a rass* when she snagged it on her hospital gown shortly after giving birth.

She kissed the baby's warm, smooth cheeks and lingered, taking in the indescribable sweetness and surge of comfort that filled her as she pressed her nose to the child's skin.

"Wake up, my Baba," she whispered into the newborn's ear as if it was a prayer.

Born 26 hours ago, Baba was not bald like the babies that smiled from diaper packages, but graced with a full head of downy black hair. The obstetrician had commented that a hairy baby was a sign of good luck in her culture. Tara didn't understand why the staff spoke about Baba's locks as if they were a rarity; she was born with the same, and so were *Nani*, Mammi and Suzie *Mosie*. Still, it was nice to imagine that her little one was destined for an auspicious future. As she delicately wiped at an area of peeling skin on Baba's forehead with a burp cloth, a shiver rippled through her.

The air conditioning in the private maternity room had switched on, sending a wave of goosebumps across her exposed breasts, making her aware of just how tender and sore they felt. Her nipples had bled a little during the last nursing session. How long has it been since then? Four hours? Five hours? Weren't newborns supposed to be fed every two hours? Was this *normal*?

Baba had been sleeping peacefully for a while now; Tara thought of the countless parent-to-be videos she'd indulged in, but for some reason, all of the "what to expect" mental notes had fled her mind.

Instinctively, her eyes searched the dimly lit room for her cell phone. The hand-me-down device had been a loyal best friend, with apps and discussion threads quelling fears and dispelling falsehoods she'd heard about pregnancy all her life with just a few words typed into the browser's search bar.

"Where *is* it?" she muttered worriedly, wondering how hard it could be to find a six-inch phone covered in blue silicone and Guyana flag stickers.

Her eyes locked onto a flashing red light at the far end of the bed, almost hidden under the thin hospital blanket. De damn thing *had* to be all the way 'foot side til she, and on top of that, *low battery*. She tightened her grip on Baba, stretched her leg out, and attempted to nudge the phone with her toes. After a few tries, she was still coming up short; impulsively, she lunged forward with her free hand to grab it.

Blazing pain.

The phone clattered to the floor. Tara sucked in air through her teeth as shockwaves ran down her legs.

"Ow Gaad! Oh, meh, the ummah. Ow..." she whimpered through clenched jaws.

The stitches that held her torn perineum together had caught onto the bulky postpartum pad pasted onto her hospital-issued white mesh underwear. An instant surge of searing anger coursed through her body, lasting only a few seconds. Molten resentments bubbled below the surface and threatened to spill out of her. She felt as if she was being suffocated by intense exhaustion that she couldn't possibly have prepared for, but how was she supposed to navigate these new emotions?

After the birth, a doctor who she hadn't met before had pressed upon her belly and checked her bloodied orifices as a group of bright-eyed residents stood around her bedside. The doctor remarked to them, "She's a textbook example," and they scribbled feverishly on their notepads in response. They spoke about her, but not *to* her. She never saw them again.

The first shift nurse had scolded Tara for falling asleep during a feeding session, brusquely taking Baba out of her arms, placing her into the clear plastic bassinet by her bed, and wheeling it away for a "Temperature Check." Baba was brought back two hours later. In hindsight, the nurse's concerns were valid, but the heavy-handedness left Tara feeling incompetent. The second shift nurse had displayed clear skepticism saying, "You gave birth without meds, and *now* you want them?" when Tara had asked for some relief from the uterine contractions that left her breathless every time she breastfed.

Tara didn't believe that she deserved to be criticized for her inexperience; all she desired was to be close to her child, to be shown some empathy, and at present—to get her phone off the floor—but she dared not to press the red "Call" button on the bed rail for fear of which nurse she'd encounter next.

The stinging between her thighs subsided to a dull ache as she looked adoringly at the soft bundle still safe in her arms. It scared her how still and serene Baba was. She seemed almost *too still* and *too serene*. Was she... breathing?

Tara stared intently at Baba's chest, but she couldn't focus. She thought she saw the rise and fall of the blanket, but what if her eyes were playing tricks on her? She placed an index finger under the baby's nose and checked for a breath as she held her own.

She waited.

A moist wisp of air tickled her finger as Baba exhaled, sighing quietly. Filled with immense relief, Tara covered the baby's wrinkly hands with kisses. Her eyes brimmed with emotion and she offered her breast once more, but Baba turned her head away with eyebrows twitching as if to say, "Leff meh alone."

Tara lifted the baby out of the swaddling and opened the snaps on her one-piece outfit. She placed the unclothed child directly onto her chest and covered them both protectively with the blanket. As Baba nestled comfortably in between her bare breasts, Tara caressed her back with an even, light touch.

Skin to skin.

Since her birth, Baba only nursed for a few minutes each time and Tara wasn't entirely sure she was getting much milk from her breasts. Maybe she needed to accept that breastfeeding might not be for her. She had heard of many new parents who weren't able to breastfeed for one reason or another. Yet with formula, their babies were now sturdy, solid *pickney*.

Tara was willing to choose formula feeding if needed. It was readily available and she and Rohan, via video chats, had already chosen the brand they would use— "Specifically formulated with proteins and inspired by the chemistry of breastmilk." As long as Baba was fed and healthy that was all that mattered.

At her baby shower three months ago, the curious and well-meaning guests had asked Tara all the customary questions: What will you name the child? Co-sleeping or crib? Breastmilk or formula? When she casually answered that she was going to breastfeed if she was able to, she noticed the exchange of glances and subtle smirks that circulated around the room.

"So I guess yuh guh be home for a *while* den. Yuh *cyan'* go back to wuk fuh now!" Big-bellied Uncle Roy said with a chuckle as he pointed to his own chest.

Tara had forced an uncomfortable smile as the family broke into a discussion about *bress*. Glasses clinked, laughter filled the air, and at the end of the conversation, even Mammi and Daddy reluctantly agreed with the crowd that breastfeeding was "Old Fashioned" and "Would only tie her down."

According to Rohan's *poowah* Aunty Pearlie, "Yuh barn hay. 'Merica people na gee bubbie! In abee time abeedeez na geh chaice. Ayuhdeez young people gah *chaice*! Dis time na lang time, gyal. Yuh too young fuh stretch yuh bubbie like ah' dah."

Lang bubbie or shart bubbie, Tara felt that she wanted to at least *try* breastfeeding until she was sure her body was fated to take one path over the other. Anything was possible in this "Fourth Trimester;" after all, she couldn't have predicted any of the twists that she had experienced with labour and delivery.

By the time the taxi had dropped her at the hospital's emergency entrance and sped away, she was already dilated eight centimetres, bracing against the cold glass doors on her forearms and resisting the urge to push. There was no time for paperwork, an epidural, or anything except to be carted away in a wheelchair straight to the birthing suite as her body threatened to tear itself open.

As Tara and Baba now rested in tranquillity to the hum of monitors and muffled conversation coming from the patient's room next door, her mind wandered to stories she had been told, tales of relatives giving birth on freshly-daubed bottom house floors or while in the backdam during planting season. It all sounded so traumatic. Her second-degree tears were testament to the ordeal she had gone through, yet it almost didn't feel like much of an accomplishment. Perhaps it was a feat by modern-day standards, but what about all those who came before her?

What did a child of immigrants, a millennial born in Queens, New York, privileged enough to give birth at a prestigious hospital on the

Island, know of pain and suffering? What were the pangs of childbirth
when her ancestors had endured cuss and cane and cutlass for generations?

Tara paused for a moment as the answer to her questions cooed and
smiled involuntarily. *Baba.* Everything...everyone...had led up to *this* point.
Their blood flowed within her, full of new life and possibility. She embodied
so many familiar and distinct ancestral features all at once. She had Rohan's
eyes, Tara's lips, Aji's high and proud cheekbones, *Aja*'s knees that slightly
bowed, Nani's nose that flared ever so slightly, and Nana's chin without the
dimple.

Tara recalled a fuzzy mix of hearsay, conjecture, and spotty details
about distant ancestors: Nani's great-grandmother was a white lady.
Somebody's *mamoo* was a drunk man, turned *sadhu*. As a very young girl,
Aja's grandmother travelled on a ship from India to Guyana. The
contract-bound travellers were called *Jahajis* and the ocean they travelled
across was the *Kala Pani*. Those terms were foreign words to Tara, newly
discovered as she took to scrolling social media posts with one hand, folding
baby shimmies direct from Port Mourant market with the other.

Those long nights alone in the apartment on Hillside Avenue,
heavily pregnant and pining away for her Rohan, were torture, but slowly
unpacking the barrel of items he had shipped for her and his unborn child
was therapeutic; she knew he had carefully chosen every vest and toy with his
very own calloused hands.

Rohan. Ten years later, the highlight of her teenage summer
vacations in Guyana, he was the love of her life, her partner in marriage, and
now Baba's daddy. He lived with his parents, older brother, and sister-in-law
in the village of Tain in the Corentyne. A wealthy family who had made their

fortune as owners of rice and lumber mills. Rohan couldn't wait for his upcoming immigration interview appointment; all he wanted was to "Get Tru" and be reunited with his wife in New York. Yet, it worried him that his usually supportive parents had lost interest in his U.S. bride and the birth of their first grandchild. Ever since the day Farah Bhoujie returned home from the private hospital up the road, sonogram picture in hand, Ma and Pa had made it clear that they would be exclusively doting over Big Buddy's manifesting legacy within her baby bump.

Rohan's family was complicated, but Tara's circle wasn't immune from life's complexities either. Mammi couldn't get any leave from her live-in job taking care of the bed-ridden 'ole man in Park Slope Brooklyn, whose family paid her well. Daddy was always off at the racetracks, alternating between Belmont and Aqueduct depending on the time of year—afterward going from dis fren' garage to dat chach basement, sporting until the bottles were empty. Even Tara's best friends and coworkers had apologetically explained that they couldn't come to the hospital between their careers and familial responsibilities, but would soon visit her at home.

At that moment, Tara's loneliness was unfathomable.

Hot, heavy tears fell from her sleep-deprived eyes as she surrendered to *all of it* and cried silently, her shoulders all of a sudden feeling heavy and tired. She wanted to sleep. She wanted to scream. She wanted to be held and fed and pampered. Her teardrops snaked their way down to the point of her chin and dropped onto Baba's tiny fingers.

As Tara *suskayed*, her breath coming out in ragged sobs, Baba made a sound to signal her discomfort and Tara scooped her up into the cradle hold again, letting the child's love envelop her.

"Come na Baba, it's *bobo* time," she called out hoarsely while drying her eyes.

She gently grasped the back of Baba's neck and tilted the newborn's head backward, attempting to coax her to open her mouth once again. The child stirred and yawned this time, her perfect lips quivering a bit. With one hand, Tara massaged her breasts, first the right, then the left, flattening, kneading, and squeezing until colostrum readily dripped from her nipples.

As if she was rousing from a centuries-long slumber, Baba opened her eyes and squinted, the fragrance of *home* on Tara's skin provoking unbearable hunger. She fussed and let out kitten-like cries of frustration as she searched for the source of the attractive scent. Baba swept her cheeks across Tara's breasts from side to side fervently until she found the nipple. She widened her mouth and latched, sucking noisily. Tara winced from the discomfort. She heard the voice of the lactation specialist from the breastfeeding app echo in her mind, "Bad latch! Break the suction and try again."

Tara took her pinky finger and gently pried Baba's mouth open until she heard a faint "Pop," releasing the suction. Baba unlatched from the nipple and started to complain shrilly once more. Her cries were not only endearing; Tara noticed that her nipples tingled and her breasts seemed to feel fuller the more the baby cried. She was fascinated by the ways her body responded to the child, and the child to her.

"Yes yes, cry lil bit na. Open yuh lungs, Baba," Tara lovingly teased.

She pulled the hospital gown completely off her shoulder and it fell down to her waist, revealing her still-puffed belly and stretch marks that radiated from her navel. She held onto her left breast and pressed down, with a swollen, cracked nipple peeking out from in between her forefinger and thumb. She held Baba's head and guided her toward the beads of opaque honey milk that were dripping down her breast.

Tara gasped. De ting still hurt bad, but not like before. Why wouldn't it? Her body was still getting used to the way Baba's little mout' a pull-pull she bubbie, not in the lover's hungry way, but something entirely different; there was an innocence and level of trust that frightened and intrigued her. She could feel the rhythmic pulling and swallowing that indicated a successful latch, the milk rushing into Baba's mouth and nourishing her lil' body.

Tara furrowed her brows within a minute as the uterine contractions started up again. They continued throughout the nursing session, the intensity ranging from period cramps to Braxton-Hicks type that ebbed and flowed. She remembered reading that the sensations were due to the natural release of oxytocin and tried to regulate her breathing. Tara imagined her organs rearranging themselves within her belly in the spaces left behind by her shrinking uterus.

The pain finally dissipated when Baba dramatically unlatched and drifted limply into another deep sleep session. She was fed. She was content. Tara wiped the sides of Baba's relaxed and milk-drunk mouth, noticing a slightly sweet aroma as the baby exhaled.

The liquid gold that flowed from her body was apparently as sweet as sugarcane.

There was a knock at the door and the third shift nurse walked into the hospital room. Tara froze in anticipation of harsh words or sneers from the woman who approached her.

"Good evening! I'm starting my shift now. How are you and baby doing?" asked the nurse, with the slightest hint of a Caribbean accent

"We're doing alright, thank you," Tara smiled shyly as she covered her nakedness with her hospital gown.

"Oops. Almost stepped on it," the third shift nurse said as she bent down, picked up Tara's cell phone from the floor, and handed it to her without a trace of judgement. Her demeanor was so calm and open, so different from all the others.

"How's breastfeeding coming along? You seem to be doing great, but you still can try the formula," the nurse said matter-of-factly as she wheeled a machine toward the bed and checked Tara's blood pressure.

"Oh... I think... I'll keep nursing," Tara responded timidly.

"Sure, you tell me what *you* want to do." The nurse paused and smiled before continuing, "It's alright to rest every so often. I promise you, the baby will be fine in the bassinet. Just so you know, before you're discharged, we'll do a routine mental wellness assessment to make sure we address *any* concerns you might have. I know it's not easy, honey."

Rest. What I want. Mental wellness assessment. Concerns. Honey!

Tara paused to look at the third shift nurse's name tag and then back up to her well-meaning eyes. She felt a tightness in her throat. She tried to hide her emotions, but she couldn't hold in the immense gratitude she felt for this stranger who had made her feel more supported in a few minutes than she had felt in months.

"Thank you... *Kala*. Baba and I would like that very much."

Mek Pickney, Mind Pickney
Angelica Razack-Francis

These past nine months have allowed me to reflect on motherhood. I found myself thinking about the women in my life and what they mean to me. As a new mother, I now feel the weight of my daughter's head on my chest. The weight of the responsibility I have as a mother and to define my role as a mother in her life.

Yes, meh mek pickney.

She came from me. I made her, but she doesn't owe me anything. She didn't ask to be born. I have the responsibility of taking care of her, loving her, and making sure she has everything she needs.

My mother, her mother, and perhaps even her grandmother viewed children as chattel. Dem mek pickney and that pickney belonged to them. They were to be seen, not heard, and expected to be obedient. At the same time, my mother and her mother worked hard to have successful careers and have a better life. They allowed someone else to mind their pickney. I have the privilege, the responsibility and the willingness to actually mind meh pickney.

This is a privilege that I choose not to give to anyone else. Not a relative or a paid nanny, just myself and her father. Neither of us is in a position where we need to leave our daughter in order to set up a new life for her. Yes, they say it takes a village, a community, and a family to raise a child, but I still felt the absence of my mother, and I am sure she felt the absence of her mother when she left Guyana to come to America to set up this better life.

Dem mek pickney, but dem didn't mind dem.

The role of minding pickney was given to my aunt, who connected me to my roots through her food, language, stories, and when she would "Touchy" the evil eye away. The role of minding pickney was also given to my paternal grandmother. She showed me love through support. She was my cheerleader, always in my corner. She connected me to my Islamic and Indo-Caribbean roots through family functions, readings, her cooking and her singing.

When I look at my daughter in her big, beautiful, brown eyes, I wonder what her expectations are of me—if she has any at all. I wonder what motherhood will look like to her.

Meh, mek pickney, but now I have the responsibility and the privilege to mind this pickney. I have the responsibility and privilege to shape what motherhood will look like to her.

Motherhood is more than mek pickney, mind pickney.

My pickney's life is her own. She does not belong to me. She is not chattel. She is a little person. An infant. When she cries, she is not bad. She is not spoiled when she falls asleep in my arms and sleeps with me. She is human.

I will mind this pickney. I will love this pickney. I will nurture and support this pickney. I will provide a safe space for this pickney to be herself and to thrive.

Meh, mek pickney. Meh, mind, pickney. Meh, love meh pickney.

Glossary

Achar: Pickled condiment made with masala

Aja: Paternal grandfather

Ajee/Aji: Paternal grandmother

Ayodhya: An ancient city of India, it is the birthplace of Rama and the setting of the great epic

Bajans: Devotional song with religious theme or spiritual ideas

Bhaji: Spinach

Bhariaat: Wedding Procession

Bhouji: Brother's wife

Bora: Long Beans

Channa: Chickpeas

Chach: Father's brother

Chowtals: A form of folksong of North India's Bhojpuri region, sung during the Phagwa or Holi festival

Chutney: A music genre created by East Indians with roots in Bhojpuri folk songs

Cook-up: Traditional one-pot Guyanese rice dish

Coolie: A low-wage laborer, typically of Asian descent

Creole: Language representing the Caribbean's hybrid cultures

Cunumunu: A stupid person

Cutlass: A large flat-bladed knife

Desi: People, cultures, and products of the Indian subcontinent and their diaspora

Dhal: Split peas cooked until softened and thick

Dulaha: Groom

Dulahin: Bride

Diwali: Hindu festival of lights

Dupatta: A shawl traditionally worn by women in India to cover the head and shoulders

Geera: Roasted and ground cumin seeds

Gilbaka: A scaleless saltwater fish found in the muddy sea bottoms of coastal rivers from Guyana

Haldi Doodh: A comforting drink made with milk, turmeric and warm spices

Indenture: After the abolition of slavery in the Caribbean, the British brought Indians under contracts to work the plantations

Jahaji: Ship brother

Jhandi: Flag

Jharay: To remove the "Evil Eye" using a pointer from a broom

Jhun-jhun-nee: A cramp in your leg from being in the same position for too long

Jumbie: Spirit of a dead person, typically an evil one

Kala: Maternal aunt

Kala Pani: Indian ocean or "Dark Waters."

Kohl: An ancient eye cosmetic, traditionally made by grinding stibnite for use similar to that of charcoal in mascara

Kurti: A long-sleeved, collarless tunic

Lehenga: A form of ankle-length skirt worm in India

Licks: A beating

Lota: A small-sized vessel made of brass, copper or plastic used to cleanse oneself

Mamee: Mother's brother's wife

Mandir: Hindu Temple

Mamoo: Mother's brother

Marr: Water collected after straining the rice

Maticoor: A female-centered ritual meant to instruct a bride to be on sexual matters

Mashramani: An annual festival that celebrates Guyana becoming a Republic in 1970.

Metemgee: A thick soup or stew made with root vegetables cooked in a rich coconut milk broth

Mosie: Father's sister

Mridangam: A double-sided drum whose body is usually made using a hollowed piece of jackfruit wood

Nana: Mater grandfather

Nani: Maternal grandmother

Pandit: A Hindu priest

Phagwah: An annual Hindu Festival of Colours celebrating the arrival of Spring

Pickney: Creole word for 'child.'

Poowah: Father's sister

Puja: Hindu religious ceremony

Raksha: Celebration of the sacred bond between siblings

Ramayana: An ancient Sanskrit epic which follows Prince Rama's quest to rescue his beloved wife Sita from the clutches of Ravana.

Rass: An expression of shock, surprise, frustration, or annoyance

Soca: A genre of music that uses Afro-Caribbean rhythms of traditional calypso with the music of India and dancehall beats

Sadhu: A holy person who has renounced the worldly life

Suskayed: To draw in breath suddenly or gasp while crying

Tawa: Circular utensil used to make roti

Tikka: Dot placed to ward off "Evil Eye."

Acknowledgements

When I first had the idea for what is called the first volume in the Two Times Removed series, I never would have imagined how my life would change. During the months of writing, editing and learning about publishing, I didn't think much about things like marketing or publicity for the book. I wanted to share stories. That was all. My only wish was that Two Times Removed would be a positive contribution to Indo-Caribbean literature and those who read it would feel seen and heard. To every reader, I want to give my sincerest thanks. There will never be enough words or a perfect way to express my gratitude. To every person who shared a beautiful photo of their book, I saved and screenshotted it. To every person who sent me a kind message, letting me know what the book meant to them, your words have stuck with me and motivated me every day to continue doing this week. To everyone who reached out to me offering their help and resources to promote the book, thank you for seeing the potential in Two Times Removed. It is an honour and privilege to have such a wonderful community.

To each of the contributing writers (Saira, Anna, Chelsea, Michelle, Amanda, Aaron, Josh, Jamie, Nalini, Jaimini, Alyssa, Alisha, Nadia, Savita, Anjali, Samantha and Angelica), I am so proud of all you. Each of your stories was personal, vulnerable and impacted me when I read them. I felt seen. I felt my family's experiences represented. I knew our community would share those same feelings. I felt like each of you had carved a unique space for yourself in history. I thank you all for wanting to be part of this project and trusting me with your work. Your voices are needed and will certainly be heard loud and clear. I'm so excited to see what the future holds for all of you.

To Chelsi, thank you for designing yet another beautiful cover. You never fail to blow me away with your talent.

To my parents, thank you for being you. So much of my inspiration to write comes from you and your stories. Our late-night chats are my favourite thing about this phase in life where I am no longer a child, yet still your child. Thank you for sharing stories with me, staying up a little longer, and supporting me every step of the way. I love you both and hope you're proud.

To my Yvano, my best friend and my love, thank you for taking the time to sit with me and help flesh out the ideas in my head. These conversations so often bring me clarity and get me back on track when I feel stuck. Outside of the productive value, sitting with you and talking will always be my favourite thing to do.

To my grandma, Sita, who is my second mother and another inspiration to me. Thank you for your unconditional love, for calling me to play the latest chutney songs, reminding me to be proud of my culture, and for the yummy food I look forward to every week.

To my little brother Jalen who looks at me with the kindest eyes. I never knew how much I needed you until you came into this world. You inspire me to live life with an open mind and see the world in new ways. I hope one day we can sit and read these books together.

To my grandparents in heaven. I wish you were here to see this. I know you'd be so proud.

About the Editor

Tiara Jade Chutkhan is a book blogger, writer and editor born and raised in Toronto. Her love of literature led her to begin blogging and sharing her reads in 2019. Through her platform, Tiara strives to promote diverse and culturally specific literature. Her blogging has allowed her the opportunity to review books for HarperCollins, Penguin Random House, Simon and Schuster and Dundurn Press. Tiara's Indo-Caribbean heritage is the focus of most of her written work and she strives to create representation for her community through her projects.

Following the release of her first book, *Two Times Removed: An Anthology of Indo-Caribbean Fiction*, in May 2021, Tiara had the opportunity to speak on several CBC radio stations, including All in a Weekend and In Town and Out. In October 2021, she was featured on the debut episode of CBC's "Rediscovering Culture" series.

Her work has been published in the Caribbean Camera, Brown Gyal Diary, Write Magazine, Caribbean Collective Magazine, and Brown Girl Magazine. *Two Times Removed Volume II: Indo-Caribbean Stories of Love, Resilience and Exploration* is her second book.

❀ Connect Online: ❀

www.tiarajade.com

@bookwormbabee

About the Contributors

Saira Batasar-Johnie locates herself as a Brown, Indo-Caribbean-Canadian cisgender woman of Indo-Caribbean/South Asian/Indian descent and first-generation settler in T'karonto/Toronto, Ontario, situated on the territory of the Anishinaabe, Mississaugas of the New Credit and Haudenosaunee Peoples, with recognition to "The Dish With One Spoon" wampum and Treaty 13. Saira's parents were immigrants escaping violence, oppression and poverty in Guyana and Trinidad. Saira is a Child and Youth Care Worker as well as a mom, wife, daughter, sister and friend. Saira is passionate about bringing the history of Indo-Caribbeans to the new generation of young people in the diaspora. She hopes to educate young people with her words and inspire them to continue their journey of understanding themselves in this world. Connect further with Saira on Instagram @saira.batasar.johnie.

Anna Marie Chowthi was born in Guyana and immigrated to Toronto, CA when she was three. She has an educational (B.Com) and professional background in Business Management with 10+ years in Corporate Canada. She's the founder of Merge Project Management and Leadership (@mergepml), a boutique leadership consultancy in Toronto, CA, where she was nominated for the 2021 and 2022 RBC Women's Entrepreneurship Awards.

She's the Creator of Savouring the Indo-Caribbean, a platform supporting a thriving Indo-Caribbean community. She's the Writer at Conscious Womaning (@consciouswomaning), a blog supporting our intentional living. She sits on the Steering Committee of the Indo-Caribbean Organization Network (@icontogether), whose work brings representation and meaningful initiatives to the Indo-Caribbean community in Canada.

She's family-oriented, a lover of conscious reggae music, nature and cultural traveller, and enjoys cooking and eating Indo-Caribbean/Caribbean foods. She's an advocate for wellness and practices various Vedic and ancient Indian philosophies and tools like meditation, pranayama, yoga asana and Ayurveda.

Chelsea DeBarros recently graduated from Hofstra University with a Bachelor's degree in Sociology and Criminology. Born and raised in South Queens, New York, to Guyanese parents, she is making an impact in the Guyanese American community as an author with her in-progress non-fiction book that reveals the untold stories of three undocumented Guyanese, their 'backtrack' journeys to America, and how their American identities helped them prevail in a world set against them. Chelsea's goal is to earn her Master's degree in Social Work to continue supporting her community as a voice for the most vulnerable populations. Follow Chelsea's book writing journey on Facebook and Instagram @backtrackjourneys.

Michelle DeFreitas was born and raised in Scarborough, Ontario. She founded Mangoes and Masala (@MangoesandMasala) to preserve Guyana's rich history and culture and provide others with a safe, online platform to explore their cultural identity. Michelle is currently pursuing her Paralegal Licence from the Law Society of Ontario. She enjoys cooking, dancing, reading, and writing short stories in her free time. Michelle hopes to continue to educate others about Indo-Caribbean culture and create more representation through her writing.

Amanda DeJesus is from Brooklyn, New York. She holds an MA in Clinical Psychology from Teachers College, Columbia University, with a concentration in Spiritual Mind/Body practices. She loves malty, robust black teas touched with delicate florals like orange blossom, probably because it reminds her of being ethereal, but grounded. She also loves planting herbs & flowers and beautiful baking things with them, fog, 90's grunge bands, Popeyes chicken and Bridgerton. She hopes to be a blessing of great love as often and to as many as she can before she leaves this place because she believes it's one of the best things we can be while we're here.

Aaron Ishmael was born and raised in Queens, New York. After a few college plays and penning the web series *Phrenic* for Caffeinated Cow productions, Aaron went on to work with Flat Tire Productions, whose mission was "Giving a voice to West Indians through theatre, video and film." Debuting on stage in Neil Simon's *The Odd Couple*, he continued with Flat Tire by co-starring in their popular sitcom *Liberty Avenue Singles* that ran for two seasons, of which he co-created/co-wrote with his dearly departed mentor and friend, Frankie Sooknanan. During those times, he toured with Flat Tire's sketch comedy show *Buttahflap*, providing "Fresh-baked West Indian comedy" to various Indo-Caribbean communities in New York, Minnesota, Florida & Canada. Aaron's current passion shifted from giving life to words on a page (acting) to creating life with words on a page (writing). Aaron is employed as a Program Manager at a Global Media Company in his professional life. He currently resides with his wife, daughter, and countless story drafts are impatiently waiting to be written. You can follow him on Instagram at @aaron.ish.mael

Josh Jaipaul, Co-Founder of Healing In Colour, is driven to help others unlimit themselves by realizing that they are first and foremost human. He intentionally prompts us to question the performative aspects of our existence, reminding us that we are in control of our lives. A life coach, author, podcast host, men's group facilitator, entrepreneur and insurance consultant, to list, but a few hats, Josh has become passionate about connecting with his Guyanese heritage and correcting the narrative around and within the Indo-Caribbean community. He embraced the opportunity to contribute to this anthology as a way to honour his paternal grandmother's journey, from which we are all likely to draw parallels.

Seeing the need for men to have safe spaces to discuss, acknowledge and evolve beyond the traditional expressions of masculinity, Josh founded Unmaskyoulinity, which develops content and retreat experiences to help men step out from the box that many live diligently inside of.

Jamie Langford was born to a Grenadian mother who immigrated to England and later California. Jamie is a clinician in California. She received her doctorate in social work from the University of Southern California and is also a licensed marriage and family therapist. Through qualitative and quantitative research, she is currently exploring the issues and implications for social work practice as it relates to second migration.

Nalini Mahadeo a first-generation Toronto-born and raised Guyanese woman, affectionately known as Nelly. After a long hiatus from her life in media and television production, she is now resurrecting her first love of storytelling. By using her own experiences, Nelly hopes to bring a fresh voice and build perspective to the complex mysteries of the Indo-Caribbean people with a special focus on balancing the old world mentality and breaking the cycle of generational trauma.

This is Nelly's first published work. Aside from her blogging experience, her words previously appeared on Brown Gyal Diary and Jubsies.

In addition to writing, Nelly is a single mom who works full time in Finance and also spends her time designing and creating handmade jewellery for her own brand, Sassy Sheek. She recently launched her own site www.talkmehname.com where she hopes to create a hub for open expression.

Jaimini Mangrue is a Guyanese-Canadian who was born in Scarborough, Ontario.

After completing an Honours Bachelor of Arts in English, Media Studies, and French from the University of Toronto, she worked as a post-secondary English as a Second Language instructor in Montreal, Quebec. Upon her return to Toronto, she decided it was time for a career change and enrolled in a Bachelor of Science in Kinesiology and Health Science program at York University. She is now a Registered Kinesiologist with interest in promoting the preventative and rehabilitative physical and mental benefits of exercise, especially to at-risk groups who may not have had access to health education.

Her love of literature and writing has stayed constant throughout her life, sparked by reading anything she could get her hands on from a young age and deciding that she wanted to be an author all the way back in Kindergarten.

Aside from her interests in content creation and writing, she is also a 5th-degree black belt in Tae Kwon Do, runs a small business on Etsy, and is a lover of all things aesthetically pleasing.

Alyssa Mongroo is a recent law school graduate of New England Law Boston. She has a BS in Criminal Justice and strives to mend the blurred lines between the Indo-Caribbean community and the South Asian community, especially with regard to the legal field. Alyssa is interested in owning her own makeup company one day and hopes to start a scholarship for Indo-Caribbean girls interested in law school.

Alisha Persaud's earliest literary pursuit involved a grade school assignment to create an animal origin myth and a terribly predictable paragraph about black and white horses named Zelda and Barbra. Thankfully, she redirected her creative energies into other storytelling outlets like Indian Classical and Bollywood dance. This led to stage and film acting, which lured her back to writing - specifically scripts - with Flat Tire Productions. This NYC-based group, of which Alisha is a founding member, is dedicated to creating opportunities for Indo-Caribbeans to be seen and heard on stage, on film, and on video. Professionally, Alisha holds a BA in Communications/Political Science and a Juris Doctor. She continues pursuing and celebrating artistic expression through choreography, dramaturgy, graphic arts, and wordsmithery from her hometown of Queens, NYC. Join her on Instagram @stagenamealisha.

Nadia C. Persaud is a Women's Fiction writer from Brampton, Ontario. She is the daughter of Guyanese farmers who immigrated to Canada and holds a BA in *Rhetoric, Media and Professional Communication* from the *University of Waterloo*. Her love for writing and storytelling began the day she learned how to read. It's led her to write articles for the *Toronto Caribbean Newspaper* and blog for the *Brown Gyal Diary*. She's currently working on a full-length novel. Follow her on Twitter (@ncpersaud) and Instagram (@ncpersaudwritenow) for more updates!

Savita Prasad (she/her/hers) is a Guyanese-American first-generation graduate student residing in Queens, New York. She graduated from Hunter College with a bachelor's degree in Biological Sciences and Psychology. Her passion for social justice led her to work with many nonprofit community organizations centred on underserved populations. Combining storytelling to promote healing, she aims to open dialogues that would lead to change. Although Savita loves to sleep, she never goes to bed on time.

Anjali Seegobin is an undergraduate student at the City College of New York, majoring in Political Science and Anthropology. She is based in Queens, New York and stems from the rich community of Richmond Hill. Growing up, writing always served as an outlet for her imagination and allowed her to advocate for important social justice issues. She is currently a contributing writer for Brown Girl Magazine, an online publication that amplifies the voices of the South Asian community. Anjali's main interest lies in advocating for her community, her passion for social justice and representing her Indo Caribbean identity.

Samantha Raghunandan was born in New York, raising her hand every time a schoolteacher asked, "Is anyone bilingual?" Deftly switching between Guyanese Creole and an American English accent evolved from a childhood "Talent" to a creative exploration of her diasporic heritage. Samantha's writing is influenced by her experience as a multigenerational caregiver and centers on the subtle complexities of marriage, parenthood, and loss. In her not-so-distant past, she's expressed her love for the performing arts as an actor with the Flat Tire Productions theater group. She enjoys reading fantasy fiction, curating family photos, and attempting to replicate that "Chatak" flavor from her parents' recipes. Samantha lovingly raises little humans alongside her husband, carrying the Spirit of her brother Michael and of Queens, NY, in her heart wherever she goes.

Angelica is an aspiring attorney, a mother, a writer. She made her first written contribution in the form of a short story/poem in Blooming Through Adversity. A graduate of CUNY Law School, Angelica has been working for BIPOC communities doing immigration and housing legal work. When she isn't working or writing, she enjoys cooking and likes to spend time with her husband and beautiful baby girl. Angelica wants to create a world where her daughter will grow up seeing her mother in spaces that we are often excluded from, whether it be literary or legal.

Until next time.

Made in United States
North Haven, CT
10 June 2022

20056071R00118